THE MAN FROM THE
FIFTH ONEIDA

HERB FRENCH

PublishAmerica
Baltimore

PublishAmerica has allowed this work to remain exactly as the author intended, verbatim, without editorial input.

Softcover 9781413769791
PUBLISHED BY PUBLISHAMERICA, LLLP
www.publishamerica.com
Baltimore

Printed in the United States of America

CHAPTER 1

Steve Glenn surveyed the jumble in the kitchen and concluded that "Babe" was getting a trifle eccentric.

Eyeing a tall stack of used plastic containers on a sideboard, he said, "Babe, you've got the finest collection of butter tubs I've ever seen. Early American, I'd say."

Babe poured some more coffee. "Now don't start picking on me. You're supposed to humor us little old ladies. Anyway, thanks for the splendid job you did outside."

"You're neither little nor old. And don't thank me until you're sure the job merits the gratitude." Steve had spent the previous afternoon and most of the morning installing a French drain, running perforated pipe in a trench from the back yard to a lower elevation in front, and covering it with crushed rock. This in an effort to save Babe's flower gardens and shrubbery from a growing swampiness.

"Babe" was Steve's favorite aunt, and he enjoyed the short jaunts from St. Louis to her home down the road in Jefferson City, Missouri. And he liked to play the role of handyman. But he had an idea there was more on her mind than a French drain when she called the other day.

Steve eyed "Babe's" old tomcat, who returned Steve's stare. "You know, I think "Scarface" is mellowing in his adult years. He actually came up and rubbed my leg a while ago. He doesn't always honor people that way."

"Yes, I noted that. 'Scarface' is a good judge of character."

Steve laughed. "Try telling that to my ex-partner. Once I was Prince Charming, and now I'm a buddy of Scarface."

"I'm really sorry you two broke up. Do you ever talk to her?"

"Oh, occasionally we talk. Pleasant conversations, actually. Kind of a "No hard feelings" sort of thing."

"Babe" reached for the coffee carafe. "You've had your share of problems lately. Why'd they let you go at the ad agency?"

"Hey, quit worrying about me. My getting sacked couldn't be helped. The law of supply and demand caught up with me the day we lost our big daddy account. An occupational hazard in the agency business." He smiled. "Also, when it came time to shrink the payroll I'm sure my name appeared in bold face caps."

"I wish you'd never left the newspaper business. Why don't you go back to the paper in St. Louis? I sure miss not seeing your bylines any more."

"'Babe', that's ancient history. Things have changed. But I'm not ruling out returning to the news side."

Scarface seized this moment to issue a "Plurrt" and jump onto Steve's lap. Steve stroked the old kitty and said, "Are you including Scarface in that family tree you're working on?"

"Maybe I should. Then maybe you'd read it. Your interest in our family tree seems rather limited.

"I'll be glad to read it when you finish it, but when will that be? I'll bet you've got enough family stuff now to fill a phone book."

"It's pretty complete. We've gone back some generations, but there's one missing link . That is, there's one link that's a total blank. Nothing known about your great grandfather, Gideon Glenn. Do you remember hearing about him?"

"Think he died in the Civil War, didn't he?"

"That could be. Do you know much about the Civil War?"

"The North won, I believe."

"That's a start. It seems Gideon disappeared during the Civil War and was never heard from again. Fanny – that was Gideon's wife – agonized over the uncertainty of the situation."

"Fanny? Why would anyone saddle a daughter with a name like that?"

"Now Steve, that was a beautiful name in those days. It wasn't used to describe a portion of one's anatomy back then. Anyway, Fanny assumed that Gideon was killed. Well, she did at first, then began to have second thoughts. Did he survive the war but didn't return?"

"That's a strange thought," Steve said. "Why wouldn't he come home?"

"Well, some soldiers did just that. Sometimes after a bloody battle there were desertions. Some would decide they wanted no more of it, and they would slip away and head west. They didn't have to go far to disappear off the map. And out west, nobody was looking for them."

"I'd think it would take a desperate man to do that," Steve said.

"Perhaps so. But there's more. The story goes that there were marital problems prior to Gideon's leaving. Your grandmother occasionally mentioned Gideon and the attempts by her mother to learn more. Nothing was ever turned up."

"Huh. You'd think some government agency would have sent her a message of some sort," Steve said. "I guess record keeping was a bit primitive in those days."

"Well, maybe not. People are learning much more about their ancestors these days, and the libraries are bulging with information about the Civil War. And then there's the Internet. That's where you come in."

"Wow! You're asking me to find the mystery man? Sounds like looking for a needle in a haystack, and you don't even know the location of the haystack. You don't have any information at all? Where was he when the war broke out? Was he one of the New York Glenns?"

"Babe" went to a bookshelf and carefully pulled down a large Bible with a dilapidated brown cover that looked to be crumbling at the edges. "Gideon's father was the one who came over from England and settled in upper New York." Babe opened the cover to a page containing notations in ink, in a delicate script.

"Here's all we have on Gideon," she said. Steve read over her shoulder: "Gideon Glenn, born July 18, 1840, near Utica, N.Y. Married Fanny McIntosh March 27, 1858. Son, Judd, born September 16, 1859. Joined Fifth Oneida, August, 1862."

CHAPTER 2

Steve shook hands with Jesse Savage in Jesse's office on the Red Campus at the University of Missouri. He had called the history professor for an appointment before leaving Jefferson City, and was pleased by the enthusiastic reception he received. Of course, Dr. Savage had a flamboyant manner about him, and maybe everyone got a hearty greeting. On the other hand, maybe he actually remembered Steve.

In his college days, some years back, Steve had written a story about Dr. Savage for the campus newspaper. It dealt in part with the idiosyncracies of the professor, who wore knickers and pedaled around campus town on a bicycle, his long hair flowing behind him. And in the fall attracted attention leading snake dances at pep rallies on football weekends.

Steve had wondered how Dr. Savage would react when the story appeared. He needn't have worried. Next time they crossed paths the professor was all smiles.

Dr. Savage tinkered with his pipe, which seemed to demand frequent attention. "So, you're embarking on a search for a relative of Civil War days. You'll enjoy that, although you may find it a bit frustrating from time to time. You'll also find that the study of ancestry and family histories is approaching a national pastime these days. A large crowd is out there walking these same paths you're about to explore."

"Well, I'm a real tenderfoot on the path," Steve said. "As I mentioned in the call, I'm trying to learn anything I can about my great grandfather, who disappeared from view during the Civil War."

"Union or Confederate?"

"I don't know, but I suppose Union. He lived in New York."

"That could make the job easier. Records for Union troops are much more complete. Some Confederate records were lost during the war, and some were destroyed late in the war and right after the war. Of course, both sides have lost records. Courthouse fires, deterioration of documents, that sort of thing."

Dr. Savage stoked his pipe. "Lived in New York. Any other information?"

"Just a note along with his birthdate that says he 'joined the Fifth Oneida'. And it gave the time as August of 1862."

"Do you know where in New York?"

"The note says he lived near Utica."

"Aha. Okay. As you may know, Mr. Glenn, both sides consisted mainly of volunteer armies, with regiments as the backbone. These regiments you might say were home-made. Home-made and home-grown. Appeals were made for enlistments, and regiments were formed at the local level.

Dr. Savage went on. "Many regiments consisted of boys from one county. Boys and men. Close friends, many of them."

"That's an army? It sounds a little like a social club."

"To begin with, it was amateurish for sure. But of necessity the soldiers in this conflict were quick learners. Very few career army men available. There were some state militia regiments, but most of them were ill equipped, and some had companies scattered around the state who had never even assembled for training as a regiment. You could say both sides were totally unprepared."

"So they were setting up new regiments. Who trained these recruits?"

"It may seem strange today, but company and regimental officers were frequently elected by the soldiers. Sometimes they were appointed by the governor. Not a good way to run a railroad, I suppose. Under this system an officer was free to rise to his own level of incompetence. But officers who didn't measure up, or coundn't hold up under fire, they didn't last long."

Dr. Savage went to a sizable bookcase located behind his desk. "It was on-the-job training for the majority of officers.

Of course, West Point graduates were in great demand, both North and South. It was a lucky brigade that was commanded by a West Pointer. He would be painfully aware of the inadequacies in leadership and would spend a lot of time instructing his officers down the line."

Dr. Savage pulled down a reference book. "All right. You said he was from Utica, New York. That's in Oneida County. Here's what probably played out. The county was getting scads of enlistments, and as the number approached 1,000, another regiment was formed. Your ancestor, then, joined the fifth regiment formed in Oneida County. And for starters it was called 'The Fifth Oneida.'"

Returning to his desk, Dr. Savage said, "The Fifth Oneida. A good starting point, I would say, would be to find out the number that was ultimately assigned to that regiment."

Steve glanced at his notes. "Does that mean I should plan on a trip to New York?"

"That wouldn't be a bad idea. But why not start the search at home?"

"Well, as I mentioned, we've found next to nothing about this man in our family files. He just disappeared from the scene."

"No, I didn't mean an internal search," Dr. Savage said. "I meant tapping the vast resources that are out there waiting for you. You're going to find an abundance of records related to the Civil War, and you can reach some of them from your desk. Just by clicking. Also, from your desk you can identify the sources that appear to have the most promise.

"I wouldn't know where to start," Steve said.

"Pension records are a good place to start. A great source of information. Some pension records contain original letters, photographs, details about the soldier's family and his occupation."

The professor prepared his pipe for a fresh load. "Now, your ancestor didn't apply for a pension if indeed he was lost in the war. But I'd look here first. Then, start searching military records. There are many sources you can tap – libraries, historical societies, state archives and the national archives, among others."

"So, the archives in New York might be able to point me in the right direction?"

"Possibly. They may be able to put you in touch with the muster rolls for that state if you go to the archives in person. Or give you the procedure for requesting information if you write. I would caution you that patience is a virtue. People are busy. They get a lot of inquiries. And the records are of great value, of course. Ancient documents are often fragile, and sometimes they won't allow you to view the original papers. In any event, no one is going to open the files and tell you to take your time. But the man in your search is in there somewhere."

CHAPTER 3

Back home in suburban Kirkwood, Missouri, Steve lit up the screen and went to his favorite search engine. After a couple of Google clicks he typed into the search box the words, "Civil War Libraries."

The Internet responded with hundreds of sources of information, from public libraries, historical societies, universities and state archives to local societies formed to perpetuate the memory of a certain regiment.

Steve singled out those sources appearing to have the most promise. All in New York. Among others, the New York Genealogical and Biographical Society, the New York State Archives and Records Aministration, the New York State Historical Society and one that particularly caught his eye – the "Sons of Union Veterans of the Civil War, honoring the memory of more than 450,000 New Yorkers who answered our Nation's call – 1861-1865."

Steve targeted E-mail addresses with a request for information on Gideon Glenn, who joined the Fifth Oneida in August, 1862. He received one response, that according to their database, Gideon Glenn was a private in the 124th New York Volunteer Infantry. Success! (Perhaps.)

Steve fired off messages to his "New York list" requesting information on the 124th New York Volunteer Infantry. A response, finally. The 124th New York Volunteer Infantry, it seems, originated in Orange County, not Oneida. With 450,000 New Yorkers fighting for the Union, Steve guessed it was hardly a coincidence to be faced with two Gideon Glenns.

Looking for one man among 450,000 New Yorkers wasn't easy. But he found a tiny consolation. Viewing one site he noted that "Over 75,000 Kentuckians fought for the Union." But went on to say that this did not include an estimated 12,000 men who saw service with other Union forces, irregular units such as the self-styled "Home Guards."

Then there were those fighting for the Confederacy, the actual number not known. Estimated between 30,000 and 40,000 Kentucky volunteers fighting for the South. Their service records, it was pointed out, were poorly kept and many of them lost or destroyed during the war. Steve decided he wouldn't want to trade with someone searching for an ancestor from Kentucky, particularly if you didn't know whether he fought for the Union or the Confederacy.

Surfing the various sources of information on the conflict, he became aware of an immense interest that the Civil War continued to generate, a fascination that seemed to be perpetuating itself. There were those like Steve, searching for a Civil war ancestor. And then add a sizable number of genuine history buffs. All combing books, pamphlets, diaries, memoirs, letters, maps, photographs, newspaper articles and files full of records.

Steve intensified his pursuit. More messages went out. He had high hopes that he would learn something from a library he had contacted in Utica, New York, the area in which Gideon Glenn was born. And located in the county where the "Fifth Oneida" originated.

As the search continued, Steve became hooked to the point where Civil War books had taken over his desk. The war, he noted, was a contradiction at every turn. Steve read that when Lincoln unveiled his Emancipation Proclamation there were riots. But the riots were in the North, not the South.

Emancipation and conscription didn't mix. To complicate matters, in some slave states Union sentiment was strong. In the North there were many people who were sympathetic with the South's cause. The state of Maryland, he read, stayed with the side of the Union only because the state legislature was prevented from convening to vote for secession.

Many men said they weren't in the war to free the slaves. They were fighting to bring the South back into the Union. Still, it was apparent to Steve that slavery was the catalyst that kept the subject of secession at a boiling point. At first, Steve couldn't understand why the two sides couldn't have prevented this volatile, emotional, deadly conflict that wreaked such havoc on the land. But he came to suspect, as one writer observed, that at the time it was like "attempting to control a tornado."

It was a costly dispute. The war lasted four years, cost hundreds of thousands of lives (estimated at more than 600,000), and wholesale destruction of property, and left a large section of the country (the South) in an atmosphere approaching the Dark Ages.

As the men started marching, the South, Steve figured, had an advantage from an emotional standpoint. They were fighting for their independence. And they were protecting their land from "the invaders." They were "defending hearth and home." That's how they saw it. Southerners, inflamed by the spirit of secession, called it "The Second American Revolution."

The North, Steve noted, had a huge advantage in manpower and manufacturing, plus a surplus of agricultural products, but the North also had one huge disadvantage. They had to do the invading.

While the mailers were failing to produce any useful responses, Steve decided to pursue the subject at a suburban library. Again he encountered a plentiful supply of subject matter, but most of it of a regional nature, with particular emphasis on a bloody engagement at Wilson's Creek, near Springfield, in his home state of Missouri.

The Wilson's Creek battle, described as the second major battle of the Civil War, was the result of an attempt by the Confederates to seize control of Missouri. This was a total surprise to Steve. He had focused on the campaigns of the Union's Army of the Potomac and the Confederate Army of Northern Virginia. All of this action occurred in the states along or close to the East Coast.

That the Civil War had extended from the Atlantic Coast all the way to points well west of the Mississippi had escaped him. There was no mention of this in the textbooks, to his recollection. Reading further, Steve learned that Missouri ranked third only to Virginia and Tennessee for the largest number of military actions fought on its soil – a total of 1,162 encounters.

Back home, Steve returned to the internet for yet another of many searches. This time he typed into the search engine, "Oneida County, New York, Civil War History." And this time he was rewarded. A web site appeared with a five-page document, titled, "History of Oneida County, New York, War of the Rebellion, 1861-1865." All of a sudden his luck was getting better.

The report estimated that Oneida County had furnished 10,000 men for the Union army during the war. Most of them quite young, no doubt. Who was left behind?

The first regiment in the county was organized in Albany, and became the 14th Infantry Regiment, New York Volunteers. The men were mustered into service in May of 1861, to serve two years. Severe losses were suffered, particularly at Fredericksburg and Chancellorsville, and the regiment was mustered out in May of 1863.

The Second Oneida, organized in Elmira, became the 26th Infantry Regiment. Composed of many men from neighboring counties as well as Oneida, it also was an ill-fated regiment, suffering severe losses at Second Bull Run, Antietam and Fredericksburg, and was dissolved May 28, 1863.

The Third Oneida became the 97th Regiment, New York Volunteers and was known just as well as the "Conkling Rifles." Organized in Boonville in Oneida County, the regiment appeared to have been everywhere, from Cedar Mountain to Appomattox Court-House and Lee's Surrender. It was mustered out July 18, 1865.

The Fourth Oneida was organized in Rome and mustered in for three years in early August, 1862. And became designated the 117th Regiment. The regiment saw early action in South Carolina, including bombardment of Fort Sumter, now in the hands of the Confederates, was also involved in the siege of Cold Harbor, Virginia, and in its last major action participated in the capture of Wilmington, North Carolina, in February of 1865. The regiment was mustered out June 8, 1865.

And then Steve's eye came to the Fifth Oneida, organized in Rome in August, 1862, under the command of Colonel Kenner Garrard and mustered into service October 10 of that year. Known as "Garrard's Tigers," it was designated the 146th Regiment, New York State Volunteers.

For a moment at least, the fog had lifted. With just a mouse click, Steve may have found his great-grandfather's regiment. But how could he be sure? And what happened to him?

CHAPTER 4

Steve discovered several ways to get information from government military records. The trick, though, was getting it done now, not three months from now.

Armed with Gideon Glenn's regimental number he was ready to go. The source of information on military service that loomed largest was the National Archives and Records Administration in Washington. Steve noted a regional office in Kansas City, Missouri, listed in the NARA web site that appeared on his screen. Just a hop across the state. But a quick phone call ruled that one out. The regional office did not have Civil War Service Records.

But he could get things started by filling out a "National Archives Order for Copies of Military Service Records," NATF form 86, and sending it to NARA headquarters. And then forgetting about it for a while. Or, how about an NATF form 85, for a search of pension records, just in case Fanny Glenn had filed for a pension? A possibility. But he still wouldn't have located Gideon.

There was one other possibility, he discovered – military service records in the New York State Archives in Albany. Their web site indicated they would "search Civil War Muster roll abstracts of New York state volunteers," for a small fee. Just fill out a "War Service Records Search Request Form," then sit back and wait.

Steve opted for all three, and ordered the forms. So now he was waiting for the forms to arrive so he could formally request a search. It was at about this point that Steve discovered he could have ordered the request forms online. That's when he decided there had to be a better way. A flight to Washington and a visit to the NARA research room? An expensive trip, and possibly for nothing. He wondered what a decent hotel room was running today in the D.C. area.

Also, he didn't look forward to taxing his skills as an amateur librarian. The military records on file would probably fill a battleship. It was his understanding every soldier's record had been painstakingly noted on cards, one card for each regiment in which the soldier served. These "Compiled Military Service Records" weren't all on microfilm, so they told him, and it took some patient navigating through the catalogs of records to reach the target.

That's how he came to know Jessica. Well, he knew her voice, anyway. It started when he hit upon a section of the NARA web site entitled, "Hire a researcher."

Out of the blue, Steve noted the phone number of a researcher near the top of the for-hire list, going by the name of "Ancestral Archives." It was an Arlington, Virginia, address. The woman who answered said she and her partner were "swamped" at the moment, but she would gladly suggest someone – a part-time researcher.

The name was Jessica Brenner, and she was a co-ed at George Washington University. After a few phone attempts Steve reached her. She said she'd like to take on the job if Steve had any information that could help her. Steve told her about Gideon Glenn's regiment.

"You sounded a little skeptical there, at first," Steve said. "Can you find him for me?"

"Probably I can," Jessica said. "You have something tangible. Some people, it turns out, don't really know whether their ancestor was wearing blue or gray."

"What sort of information do you usually turn up in these searches?" Steve wondered how much experience she had in this field.

"That depends. Military service records can be brief. If there's a pension record on Gideon Glenn, that's another matter. Interesting reading. You'll sometimes find accounts of things that happened in the family, marriage certificates, family letters, records of births, things like that."

George Washington University, Steve learned, was close to the action. Just four blocks from the White House, she had told him.

Steve was now playing the waiting game. After two days he called, and Jessica told him she had made it to the research room the afternoon before, but ran out of time before closing. She would try to get it done after classes tomorrow.

Another two days, and finally a phone call. She had found Gideon Glenn, and a copy of his military service record was on its way. Sorry, she could turn up no mention of a pension.

Steve watched the mailbox, and at last the envelope arrived from Jessica. Had he finally found his long-lost relation? He set aside the enclosed copies of records, mostly to do with "company muster rolls," and read Jessica's cryptic notation:

Gideon Glenn – 146th Regiment, New York Volunteers. Age 23 years.

Enlisted August 27, 1862, at Utica, to serve three years. Mustered in as private, Co. F, October 10, 1862. Promoted corporal March 9, 1863.

Captured in action May 5, 1864, at the Wilderness, Va; no further record.

CHAPTER 5

Gideon Glenn had decided to enlist. He was 22 and in excellent physical condition, thanks in part to a life of considerable toil on the farm. He looked like a model recruit. Unlike some of the other recruits, he also had a wife and a young son.

It was late afternoon, August 27, 1862, in the village of Utica. Gideon was casting his eye at a poster outside the recruiting headquarters:

MEN OF ONEIDA COUNTY – THE UNION IS IN DANGER!

Able-bodied recruits 18 years of age or older are sought to

fill the ranks of the 146th New York State Volunteers,

to quell the rebellion and restore the Union!

Gideon guessed that the youngster in line directly in front of him had yet to celebrate his 16th birthday. But the recruiting committee, he suspected, would approve him if he could stand there and claim he was 18.

The war was in its 16th month now, and reality was setting in. Cooler heads had come to realize that Sherman was right when he predicted that it would be a very long and costly war.

And no longer were they looking for patriots to serve for three months. Now, the enlistment term was three years.

Still, there was a circus-like atmosphere in the village. Business was suspended at 4 every afternoon, and bells rung to announce that the recruiting drive was under way. Newspapers published stirring appeals. Banners urged men to come to the aid of the Union. Bonfires, torchlight processions, brass bands and speakers, usually associated with political campaigns, stirred sparks of patriotism in the folks.

Just a week earlier 1,000 men of 1100 volunteers in the Fourth Oneida had been mustered in to the county's fourth regiment, the 117ᵗʰ New York Volunteers. The other 100 would form the start of the new regiment, the 146ᵗʰ· The county's military committee was offering a "special bounty" to each volunteer, this on top of the $50 state bounty, but it appeared no inducement was necessary. Shopkeepers, blacksmiths, harness makers, teachers, preachers, stable hands and farmers were among those willing, if not eager, to answer the call.

Gideon was told to report at Camp Huntington in nearby Rome just as soon as he could get there. He bade his wife, Fanny, and son, Judd, goodbye, with the assurance that he wouldn't be gone long. He really wasn't sure of that, but thought the odds good that the North might overwhelm the South in the not-too-distant future.

In the meantime, Gideon guessed army life might be a welcome relief from their hardscrabble existence on the farm he had taken over from his father-in-law. Not a great distance from the Adirondack Mountains, the acreage was distressingly rocky and much of it subject to erosion. The past crop year had been a disaster, starting with spring floods that delayed planting in a season that couldn't afford delays. And the current year promised little improvement.

Fanny's aging father, too ill to work the fields, was still available to pass judgment when things went wrong, and it seemed to Gideon that his negative attitude was rubbing off on Fanny. Gideon had a plan. After the war he would pack up their possessions, and he and Fanny and Judd would head for the state of Iowa. There he would claim 160 acres as a homesteader, and they could start anew. He had heard that the land there promised abundant yields, and remained fertile. And the homesteaders in Iowa had "just scratched the surface," so he had heard.

Gideon had plenty of time to think things out, in his brief stay at Camp Huntington. Drilling and parading were the main activities, and this effort was much hampered by the fact that there were only enough guns for use on guard duty. And the regiment's commanding officer, a Colonel Garrard, from West Point, had yet to arrive.

But things changed in early October, shortly after the regiment was officially "mustered in." The men responded to the order to "fall in," and strapped on their make-shift knapsacks. Along with the others, Gideon carried a haversack which he had stuffed with a fresh supply of ham and bread, intended to last for three days. They marched to cars, 25 in all, at the train station.

In Albany, Gideon marched with the men to another rail line, the Hudson River Railroad, enroute to New York City. It was nighttime, and sleeping was difficult. Some men found it easier to sleep on the floor than in the rock-hard seats. The next day, in New York, they marched from the rail terminal to the docks, where they boarded two steamers bound for South Amboy, New Jersey. On the open water, Gideon gazed in awe at the magnificent scene – the two rivers flowing on either side of Manhattan, with the city of Brooklyn, the tree-clad hills of Long Island and the Palisades of New Jersey in the distance.

On shore, they went by train to Philadelphia. There they were invited to breakfast at a place called the "Cooper Shop Volunteer Refreshment Saloon," big enough to serve an entire regiment at a time. With lady volunteers serving, the hearty meal was a gift from the city of Philadelphia, a service available to all regiments passing through on their way to Washington. Gideon suspected it was a meal to remember.

From Philadelphia, the men were sent by rail to Baltimore, and then on to Washington, DC. The morning they arrived in the Capital City they marched along Pennsylvania Avenue, past the Treasury Building and across a bridge and down a road to Arlington Heights, Virginia.

Along the road they saw thousands of cattle, sheep and hogs, closely guarded by men in the commissary department. Ambulance wagons passed the marchers, carrying soldiers to hospitals in Washington. Gideon realized that the regiment was no longer just a group of men involved in drilling, marching and guard duty. Now they were about to find out what it was like to be a part of the Union Army.

CHAPTER 6

Steve was learning much more about the Civil War than he was learning about the mysterious Gideon Glenn. He had just finished a book entitled, "A Short History of the Civil War," of approximately 350 pages, and found it both fascinating and perplexing. And, yes, he agreed it was "short," if you considered the mass of historic events that was compressed into these pages.

Part of the fascination for Civil War buffs, Steve suspected, was studying genius at work. Or something approaching genius. The ability to read an opponent's mind and set a trap. Or avoid one. Being able to skillfully maneuver 30,000 men, plus another 30,000 horses and mules, sometimes even making them vanish from sight, at least from the eyes of the enemy. On the Union side, for example, Grant, Sherman, Sheridan, Thomas. On the Confederate side, Lee, Jackson, Longstreet, A. P. Hill. For starters.

Steve found a number of Web sites with information pertaining to the 146th Regiment (described variously as the 146th Regiment Infantry, Halleck's Infantry and Garrard's Tigers). The regimental history was there in capsule form. Steve learned that the men in the regiment quickly lost their status as "rookies," when they reached Fredricksburg, a couple of months after they left camp in Rome, New York. This in December, 1862.

For much of the Battle of Fredericksburg, their first encounter with the enemy, the 146th was a witness more than participant, which was fortunate for them since the battle was a complete disaster for the Union, and many men in blue were lost. Union General Burnside would shortly surrender his command to "Fighting Joe" Hooker.

Delving further, Steve learned that the men of the 146th got their feet wet in every respect in their next encounter. This in late April and early May of 1863, at Chancellorsville. Now under the direction of Hooker, the campaign, in the words of one writer, "was begun with such promise of success, but ended in nothing more than miserable failure."

At one point in the action the regiment found themselves isolated in a position that could be flanked both left and right. This at the time that the whole Union advance had stalled. All around was heavy underbrush and impassable forests. They finally managed to fall back, but not before suffering losses. About 20 members of the 146th were killed or wounded, the first of the regiment to fall on a battlefield, and a few others were captured.

It rained during much of the campaign, and the men had little opportunity to build fires to cook food. There was tasteless hardtack. And the commissary department furnished raw meat from cattle that had been shot down. Not too tasty in the absence of a cooking fire. And to top it off, early in the campaign they had to ford the Rapidan River in waist-deep water that was still close to its icy winter-time temperature. Chancellorsville had been a sorry experience, Steve was certain of that.

Coming out of school, Steve knew next to nothing about the Civil War. It surprised him now to realize that in those days he didn't even know where it was fought. Although there was one Civil War battlefield that probably would have come to mind, even in his grade school days, if asked to name one. Gettysburg.

Now, having immersed himself in some of the triumphs and tragedies of that defining era, Steve saw Gettysburg as indeed a crucial point in history. As expressed in one of his recently-acquired books to do with the Civil War, "Gettysburg was the greatest battle in the history of the Western Hemisphere."

The action at Gettysburg made fascinating reading. And then Steve discovered that the men of the 146th Regiment, New York Volunteers, were there. It was a feeling he wouldn't soon forget, knowing a relative was playing a role in that pivotal moment in time.

Early on in his search, Steve had found that pinpointing the regiment was sometimes just part of what he needed to know to fit the players into the action. Accounts of action in or leading up to a battle often dealt with brigades, or divisions, or corps and corps commanders, rather than individual regiments.

Oddly, Steve had found information about the command structure related to the 146th regiment in a book by a Confederate. A book which he had skimmed in the local library, entitled, "From Manassas to Appomattox," by Confederate General James Longstreet.

Longstreet, in describing some of the action at Gettysburg, listed the 146th, under Colonel Garrard, as being part of the Union's Third Brigade, headed by Brigadier General Stephen H. Weed. The Third Brigade a part of the Second Division under Brigadier General Romeyn B. Ayres, and that division a part of the Fifth Army Corps, headed by Major General George Sykes. Moving up from regiment to brigade, to division, to corps.

Now, when Steve found some action involving Sykes, Ayres or Weed, he knew that in most cases he was closing in on action involving the 146th. And the three of these commanders in the Fifth Corps had encountered more than their share of the fury and the confusion that surrounded the action at Gettysburg.

Viewing maps and photos of Gettysburg, it occurred to Steve that the battleground was something like a huge theater. Unlike other battles such as at Chickamauga and the Wilderness, with dense undergrowth and terrain so heavily timbered that couriers got lost, Gettysburg was more or less wide open. With many high points that were ripe for viewing.

And what a sight it must have been when those two great armies came almost by chance to encounter one another at this tiny crossroads. There were several landmarks in this battleground theater that etched their names in history on those first three days of July in 1863.

To the west of the village of Gettysburg -- McPherson's Ridge and Seminary Ridge, where Lee made his headquarters. To the east -- Culp's Hill, south of the village, not far from where Union General Meade, Hooker's replacement, made his headquarters. And farther south -- Cemetery Ridge, followed by two rocky prominences, Little Round Top and Big Round Top, and nearby, a jumble of huge boulders that came to be known as the Devil's Den. Not to overlook the nearby Peach Orchard and the Wheat Field that played a large part in the action.

All roads in the area funneled into Gettysburg. Steve in his readings was surprised to learn that many of the Confederates were barefoot. On roads in Virginia this wasn't as tough on feet as it was on the harder-surfaced roads in the north. There were rumors that shoes were available in Gettysburg and the arriving Confederates were anxious to learn first-hand whether this was true. But instead, they ran right into advance pickets of the Union forces.

These men, they were sure, were regular troops, not militia, and they reported this to Confederate General A. P. Hill, who wouldn't believe it. He didn't think any Union forces were anywhere near. But that evening there was much excitement in the South's camp when a scout reported to Lee that the entire Army of the Potomac was indeed descending on this neighborhood.

Lee's plan at this point had been to go to Harrisburg, the capital of Pennsylvania, and seize it. That night he said, "Tomorrow, gentlemen, we will not move to Harrisburg as we expected, but will go over to Gettysburg and see what General Meade is after."

CHAPTER 7

When General Meade assumed command of the Army of the Potomac, relieving General Hooker on the evening of June 27, 1863, he was faced with the most intimidating task yet to be confronted by a Union General.

The South had invaded the North. The Confederates were 50 miles to the north of Meade's forces and were threatening to take the capital of Pennsylvania. The people were in panic. Meade must somehow divert Lee's attention away from Harrisburg.

The army was put in motion northward. The 146th got their marching orders June 29, and after a march of 15 miles camped for the night near Liberty, Maryland.

Rumors floated through the regiment as to where they were going, but it was no rumor that Lee had headed north. Gideon Glenn found it a pleasant relief to be back on friendly northern soil again. People came to their doors and waved, and some expressed their friendship in a more tangible manner, handing out fruit, bread, pies and cakes, others equipped with cold water or milk. A far cry from the hostility shown by the occasional onlookers in Virginia.

June 30, the marching resumed at 3 a.m. and continued for 23 miles. The following morning, July 1, "Day One" of the action at Gettysburg, they were awakened at daybreak. It was hot and dry, and the marchers stirred up a cloud of dust that made it difficult to breathe or see. It was a fast pace. Feet were blistered. Some men took off their shoes and stockings and carried them on the ends of their bayonets.

It was nearly midnight when they halted for good. They were now in Pennsylvania, near a village called Bonaughtown, five miles from the village of Gettysburg.

In the early morning of July 2, the order was passed to "Make coffee and fall in." By dawn they were back on the road, moving up the Baltimore Pike at a rapid gait. They crossed Rock Creek, near Gettysburg, about 7 a.m. After being brought into a wooded area, they moved toward Cemetery Hill, west of Gettysburg. They waited.

About 3 pm the word came from Colonel Garrard to "Fall In." Captains shouted out orders, and the 146ᵗʰ found themselves leading both brigade and division. Ammunition wagons raced by. They passed medical corps tents, the staff watching the passing scene. Officers shouted, "Close ranks, load as you go!"

They skirted the woods at the foot of a rocky height that came to earn the name,"Little Round Top." When they emerged from the trees they found themselves on the battlefield at Gettysburg, not far from what will forever be remembered as The Peach Orchard.

The regiment arrived in the thick of things. The Confederates were about to swarm over one Union position. The Union line ran north and south, heading southward along high ground called Cemetery Ridge. But starting with the Third Corps, commanded by General Sickles, the line jutted out to a point well to the west of the intended line of defense as planned by General Meade. This left the Third Corps vulnerable to attack from all angles. And this left the area around Little Round Top virtually unprotected.

The Confederates saw this opportunity. They shifted their attack so as to assault the Union line in front of Little Round Top. While Sickles' corps was being overwhelmed in the Peach Orchard, a regiment of Texans was skirting the foot of Little Round Top on the south side, in an effort to take the top.

Meanwhile, Gouveneur K. Warren of Meade's staff, who had been sent to take a look at Little Round Top, saw potential for disaster. From the crest he could see the whole battle being played out below. It was crucial ground, and only a handful of signalmen were there. Confederate artillery on Little Round Top could sweep the entire Union line from Culp's Hill to Cemetery Ridge.

Warren sent a message to Meade, then went for help. Encountering the 140th New York, he told the regiment's commander, Colonel O'Rorke, that it was urgent that his regiment scale Little Round Top.

Shortly Union General Weed got word to head immediately for Little Round Top. And a Union brigade headed by Brigadier General Strong Vincent was climbing the eastern side of the promontory. And none too soon. The regiment that occupied the left flank of this line, the 20th Maine, was attacked by Alabama regiments approaching from the south. The commander of the 20th Maine was Colonel Joshua Chamberlain.

Meanwhile, other Confederate troops had outflanked the Third Corps and were heading toward Little Round Top, with the Fifth Corps in their sights. Shortly, one of the men of the 146th was struck, the first member of the regiment to be killed at Gettysburg.

The 140th had reached the top, some distance to the right of Vincent's Brigade, and the men were in combat with the Texans, who had almost reached the crest. The 146th now began the difficult scramble up the northern and most gently sloping side.

Even then, the climb was not easy. To complicate matters, a battery of horse-drawn gun carriages was being brought to the top, and the men were tugging at the wheels in an attempt to help the horses gain a footing.

The 146th found total confusion at the top. The 140th was in hand-to-hand combat with the Texans, who had superior numbers before the rest of Weed's brigade managed to gain a foothold. Butts of guns and bayonets replaced bullets in the absence of repeating weapons. Also stones, which were plentiful. Colonel O'Rorke was one of the first men killed in the midst of this turmoil.

The Confederates were driven back, and General Weed set about restoring order. The flag of each regiment was placed at a prominent spot, and buglers sounded "assembly." It was almost 5 p.m. on Day 2. While the men were regrouping, General Weed was shot down, also Captain Hazlett, commander of "Hazlett's Battery" of horse-drawn guns that had been dragged to the top. They were hit by sharp-shooters in the Devil's Den, a jumble of boulders a short distance to the west of Little Round Top.

Colonel Garrard of the 146th Regiment assumed command of the brigade. Hazlett's battery, minus their old commander, was set up with a view of the action below, and the 140th was posted to the left of the battery, with the 146th to the right. Men from each regiment were sent to the bottom of Little Round Top, where they stationed themselves behind the rocks at the base of the hill.

The Confederates were making some headway up the slope in a final effort to take the hill. They first hit the skirmish line in front of the 140th New York and 91st Pennsylvania, then reached the point where the 146th New York and 55th Pennsylvania were stationed.

They were greeted with round after round of musketry. Their attack was too late. They slowly fell back, minus a great number of their men.

It was near dark, and finally it was quiet on Little Round Top. The men made themselves as comfortable as possible on ground covered with boulders and rocks of all sizes. It was, in the words of one soldier, "as poor a bivouac as you could imagine."

Cries of the wounded could be heard, and men of the ambulance corps remained busy well into the night. But after marching more than 20 miles, followed by a day of anxious waiting and a few hours of active fighting, sleep wasn't that hard to find.

On Day 3 the men were told to stay alert, but no assault was made on Little Round Top. Gideon spent the morning listening to the firing in other areas and staying partially under cover to avoid the sharpshooters in the Devil's Den. General Warren was among those wounded by their fire. Later, two companies of sharpshooters arrived on the scene and finally put an end to the Confederate sniping.

The men were now able to venture out at will. A stunning spectacle greeted the onlookers. They had a complete view of the great battlefield, Big Round Top to the south, the Devil's Den directly ahead, the Wheat Field to the right of the Devil's Den, and farther on, the ill-fated Peach Orchard. And in the distance, the gleaming guns of the Confederate artillery stretched along Seminary Ridge to the west.

Rumors were everywhere that the Confederates were preparing another attack. Their only success thus far had been wiped out – the victory north of town on the first day and the occupation of the Devil's Den and overwhelming of Sickles' position on the second.

Any guesswork should have had more to do with "where" and "when" rather than "whether." Lee had resolved to pierce the center of the Union line, viewed as the weakest link. This plan against the advice of Lee's "old warhorse," Longstreet.

For some time the South launched artillery fire from their batteries along Seminary Ridge. Then about 10 a.m. the firing ceased. Suddenly, in early afternoon, smoke and flame shot out from the Confederate positions. Then, all hell broke loose. The deafening roar of over a hundred guns. The artillery of Lee's army. Nearly 100 Union guns on Cemetery

Ridge answered, the heaviest cannonading ever heard on the American Continent.

Some shells came screaming toward Little Round Top, bursting among the rocks on the side of the hill or shrieking over their heads. Hazlett's battery, just to the left of the 146th, joined in. Gideon noticed that Colonel Garrard looked as cool as if he was witnessing a review.

But most Confederate fire was concentrated on that segment of the Union line stationed along Cemetery Ridge, doing considerable damage among the artillery batteries nearby. Finally, Meade ordered a halt to the Union firing to conserve for whatever was coming. The Confederates had slowed their barrage. Soon all was still. Heavy smoke covered the entire area.

Overlooking the battlefield atop Little Round Top, the 146th Regiment had the equivalent of front row seats in the balcony. As the smoke lifted they saw, in the distance to their right, Pickett's 15 Virginia regiments move across the fields as though on dress parade, the brigade commanders in front.

The soldiers of the South were crossing nearly a mile of open country, directly in range of the Union guns. Despite damage done to the Union batteries there was still lots of firepower, and the Confederate artillery had not made a dent in the Union infantry, the men dug in behind stone walls, breastworks and trenches.

The Confederates were mowed down, lines of men seeming to vanish. Still they came, reaching Union positions at some points, the men in blue wavering, desperate hand-to-hand conflict, before Union reserves swept down on the scene. The Confederates gave way and retreated – those still standing.

When certain it had ended, the Union troops up and down the line of several miles shouted, and some wept. The men on Little Round Top threw caps and canteens in the air, dancing and hugging in their excitement and relief that it was over.

CHAPTER 8

Steve Glenn's search through various sources of Civil War history was yielding a wealth of information on the experiences of the 146th Regiment. He was pleasantly surprised that tales of the regiment's adventures had survived so well the passage of time. But he wasn't any closer to learning the fate of his long-lost relative.

One day, while roaming the net for any additional information about the 146[th,] Steve had chanced on a Civil War chatroom in which Gettysburg was the topic. The chatroom members were roasting Union General Sickles for his decision to set up his corps well forward of the line intended by Union General Meade.

This on Day 2 at Gettysburg. The decision had left Sickles and his men out on a limb, so to speak, a disaster both for Sickles and his men. And the chatroom messages were deep into the subject.

Why had Sickles disregarded Meade's orders? On the other hand, wasn't the ground that he occupied actually higher than the position he was ordered to take? Couldn't the Confederates have taken the "Devil's Den" with or without any mistakes by Sickles?

Steve had no intention of getting into a discussion with these folks. He had no doubt that the Civil War was their passion. Probably went to lectures on Antietam or Shiloh and attended local Civil War Round Table meetings. And, when time permitted, traveled to national battlefield sites to take in the scene, or to witness re-enactments.

The message center, originally named the "Rally 'Round the Flag" chat room, had quickly evolved, in the interest of brevity, into the "Rally Chat." Only registered "Rally" users could log in, but Steve found he could monitor the postings as an "unregistered guest."

It was interesting, the cyberspace banter back and forth over the issue of General Sickles, that is until two members chose to disagree. When one member suggested that General Meade had approved the plan by Sickles to move into the Peach Orchard, this comment was branded as "idiotic." Whereupon a member called "Sarge" posted a reminder about a rule that if you disagreed with someone you must state your source, or state that this is your opinion.

This drew a comment from a member with the handle, "C. W. Buff" that defused the situation. A bit off the subject, he commented:

"I'm glad that Sickles chose to occupy the Peach Orchard because he stumbled into the path Longstreet was going to take in his attempt to occupy Little Round Top. This may be the reason Longstreet took so long to act. And my great granddaddy was one of Longstreet's boys."

As the session was winding down, Sarge posted mention that an interesting paper on the history behind today's military rank structure was available to anyone interested. Copies could be obtained from cwbuff@netscape.net.

Steve made note of the e-mail address. Here, it appeared, was a student of Civil War days and someone who was generous with his thoughts. He decided he'd like to learn more about "C. W. Buff," and sent off the following message:

"We have something in common. My great grandfather was with the 146th Regiment, New York Volunteers, on Little Round Top on Day 2 at Gettysburg. Have you ever visited the battlefield?"

And he signed the message, "Greenhorn."

When Steve went on the "net" the next morning in his apartment, there was a reply to "Greenhorn" in his in-box:

"Yes, I've been to a bunch of battlefields, and Gettysburg is as good as it gets. Well-maintained and well-preserved. Incidentally, the stone walls and barricades built by the Union boys who were on Little Round Top still stand today. I guarantee a visit to this site will transport you back in time."

C. W. Buff

Steve was now into another Civil War book, this one entitled, "A Stillness At Appomattox," by Bruce Catton, and had just finished reading about the Battle of Fredericksburg in late 1862, still early in the war. It was one of the Union's worst defeats, in which brigade after brigade stormed the high ground occupied by the Confederates. Surveying the scene in advance of the first charge, Confederate General Longstreet was supposed to have said, "A chicken could not live in that field once we open on it." The Union forces were mowed down.

With this debacle in mind, Steve sent a message to C. W. Buff:

"The more I read about the Civil War, the more amazed I am at the apparent willingness of the men to launch a charge in the face of withering fire. To advance across an open field, or a bridge, or up a hill, totally exposed – I think I might have suggested to someone that this was not a very good idea."

Greenhorn

Steve wondered what possessed these men. What terrible odds! Their next step could be their last one. But they didn't seem to waver. He didn't have long to wait before a reply appeared from C. W. Buff, addressed to "Greenhorn":

"There has been much written about how dedicated the men on both sides were to their cause. But recently historians have suggested maybe it was more a matter of comrades than cause. Many regiments consisted of men who were almost entirely from one county, perhaps two or three villages. You knew these guys. And you pretty much figured if your buddy was heading up that slope or across that bridge, so were you."

C. W. Buff

It was time, Steve decided, to come to the point. He sent off a short message:

"Where did you go to find the information you have on your Civil War ancestor?"

Greenhorn

The new cyberspace friend of Steve's was quick with a reply:

"Which ancestor? Are you talking about my great grandfather who was at Gettysburg, or my relative on the other side of the fence? My grandfather, in this case. The ancestor with Longstreet's First Corps was easy to trace. Much has been written. As for my other ancestor, I had to do a lot of digging. He no doubt spent more time ridding himself of lice than he did aiming at the enemy."

C. W. Buff

Steve fired off another message to "C. W. Buff," who had referred to himself on one occasion as "Your Confederate Pen Pal":

"If your grandfather saw little or no action in the war, how were you able to learn anything about his whereabouts and his experiences (or lack of same)?"

Greenhorn

Shortly there came a reply to "Greenhorn" that clarified the issue:

"After some digging, I was fortunate enough to find a regimental record that traced the journeys of his outfit, and mentioned on occasion the officer who headed his unit. Knowing his name helped me follow their path. It seems the regiment stayed busy ripping up railroad tracks and otherwise disrupting Union supply lines. That's the way it is in war. You do what someone tells you to do. ... So, I gather you're having trouble uncovering information pertaining to one or yours, huh?

C. W. Buff

All that Steve knew about his long-lost relative he passed along to "C. W. Buff":

I don't have much information. His name was Gideon Glenn, and as mentioned in earlier message, I had read an account that placed his regiment on Little Round Top on Day Two.

The 146th Regiment, New York Volunteers. He was captured May 5, 1864, at the Battle of the Wilderness, and that's all I know. Where can I go from there?

Any ideas?

Greenhorn

CHAPTER 9

They couldn't have picked a worse place to do battle than in the area in Virginia known as "The Wilderness," but then, nobody picked it. The battle occurred as Grant, now the commanding general, was moving the Army of the Potomac southward with intent to continue pressing Lee's forces until surrender was the only option.

The Wilderness was a gloomy and forbidding area of several miles along the Rapidan River. It was a tangle of trees and dense underbrush, and a soldier couldn't see more than a few yards in any direction. No problem hearing someone, though, if they were trying to move about in that thicket.

When Grant's forces reached this area, May 4, 1864, the idea was to slip through as fast as possible and hopefully force an encounter with Lee in open country farther south. The men were about to learn that, with General Grant, retreat was not an option. The Wilderness was in his way, and he intended to depart the area before Lee could encounter him.

Members of the 146th felt a vague uneasiness as they started down the "Germanna Plank Road" into a dense, dark forest. On the march they encountered other roads – trails, actually, but this was the only road of a north-south variety that went clear through the Wilderness.

Presently, the men came upon a crossroads and an abandoned stage station known as the Wilderness Tavern. The jungle was so thick you could almost stumble on the crossing before you saw it. Humans had deserted the area and left the vine-covered premises to the rats and spiders. The east-west road running by the Wilderness Tavern was called the Orange Turnpike, heading eastward to Fredericksburg and westward to the Orange Courthouse.

The 146th regiment was sent westward. It was late in the day and they soon reached their camping ground on the north side of the turnpike road. The men were unusually quiet that evening. They were in a jungle in enemy territory, unfamiliar both to them and their commanders, and the mood was subdued. No singing, no horseplay.

There was reason for concern. The men were rousted out at 5 o'clock on May 5, and they were boiling their coffee when an officer appeared with word that the enemy was nearby. The news passed quickly. The 146th was soon marching westward.

The regiment had orders to take position in the woods north of the pike. Decision had been reached by Grant to attack "if the opportunity presents itself," which was met with some concern by the field officers. They were beginning to suspect that the enemy was out there in sizable numbers.

What nobody knew among the Union troops was that a giant force was out there – General Ewell's corps of Confederates, nearly 20,000 men in all.

To the west, through any breaks in the trees, you could now see a large cloud of dust where the Confederate forces were forming a line of battle. The lines were so close that troops could hear the noise of trees being chopped down for breastworks. The 146th was ordered to move up and take a position at the edge of a clearing. With the order to charge, the men dashed out of the underbrush into the clearing, and were soon met with heavy fire.

They crossed a gulley, many of them reaching the woods on the other side. Both forces were firing furiously, but at what, they could rarely tell. Tree limbs shattered and underbrush caught fire. And dense clouds of smoke began to hover over the entire area.

Now, with the Rebel yell suddenly added to the din, the Confederates charged, and the Union lines, disorganized, with gaps here and there in the underbrush, began to break. The Confederates were quick to find the gaps. In the confusion, officers and men of the 146th lost track of their units. Many men tried to move back across the clearing and suddenly found themselves trapped, with Confederate forces all around them.

In just a few minutes from the time they charged across the clearing until they were forced back, the 146th Regiment was almost put out of commission. More than half the regiment was gone. Nearly 400 were killed, wounded and missing out of a total force of 600. Only ten officers out of 24 remained. Of the six officers and 184 enlisted men reported missing, most had been taken prisoner, many of them soon to be on their way to a notorious prison camp, Andersonville.

CHAPTER 10

Steve was surprised by the volume of material about Andersonville, in his first visit to the prison on the internet. His pen pal, "C. W. Buff," had suggested that Steve look into the Andersonville prison records, on the basis that many Union men captured at the Wilderness wound up there.

No matter what search he pursued ("Andersonville Prisoners of War," "Deaths at Andersonville," "Survivors of Andersonville" or "Andersonville Prison Records"), he found much written, but few specifics. Emphasis was on the sorry conditions there from early 1864, when it opened, until late fall of that year, when the last of the able-bodied prisoners had been sent elsewhere. The prison was reportedly built to hold up to 10,000 prisoners. By July it was jammed with more than 30,000 and may have housed as many as 45,000 total.

An open-air stockade, the men were exposed to all the elements, cold nights some of the time, and the hot Georgia sun almost all the time. They were on starvation rations. A stream running through the stockade served as both a sewer and the only source of drinking water. The area was grossly overcrowded. Men were dropping from dysentery, scurvy, malaria and exposure, and many were simply starving to death.

Steve was learning more than he wanted to know about Andersonville. But learning whether one man in a regiment in upper New York had indeed been a prisoner was not easy. Steve also noted there was room for error. One descendant attempting to trace a Civil War ancestor had turned up information that the relative had died of malnutrition at three different Confederate prisons, Andersonville included.

Searching the many web sites dealing with the infamous prison, Steve found one with an "Andersonville Prisoner list," and turned up one Glenn -- Aaron M., from Indiana. Along with rank, date and location of capture, and that he died at Andersonville.

Steve entered the name, "Gideon Glenn," and received a reply, "Sorry, no records were found matching your search criteria."

Pursuing further, Steve finally uncovered one outstanding source of information on the subject – the Andersonville National Park Service. Their prison records accounted for about 32,000 of the men who had been sent there, and the 32,000 were in a database at the Andersonville park site. This was the last word on the subject, and Steve guessed this was his last chance. He went online to the database, and waited.

If Gideon didn't show up here, should he scrub the mission? What a painstaking chore it must have been to compile a record of 32,000 prisoners! After all, there was no "guest register" for these men. The database was said to be the most comprehensive listing of the Civil War era. In fact, many prison camps, he was learning, had records of deaths only. No records of survivors. And in some cases no records at all.

Besides, why was he believing that Gideon was ever a prisoner? The record said, "Captured in action." Maybe he escaped. It happened frequently. There were many opportunities to slip away from a company of men on the move. Grant even paroled an entire Confederate army at Vicksburg, "on their honor to go home and cease fighting," mainly because Grant had no way of feeding them. Maybe Gideon headed west, as some disillusioned fighters did, and as Fanny Glenn seemed to have suspected was possible.

Steve was finally rewarded for his perseverance. He received the following message concerning "Andersonville Prison Records, from the Andersonville National Park":

Company CodeName

F 40358 GLENN, GIDEON

A glance at the legend told Steve that the numbers 10,000 to 29,999 were for those "Buried at Andersonville." Numbers 30,000 to 39,999 – "Reportedly died at Andersonville but lack any record." And 40,000 to 49,999 – "Left Andersonville Alive."

Steve stared at the message. Gideon Glenn had indeed been at Andersonville! And he left Andersonville alive? He had been missing for a century and a half, and now it turns out he was a POW. And duly recorded. Wouldn't it have been of some comfort to Fanny Glenn to have known?

Why didn't word reach the Glenn family? But then, there was no database at Andersonville when Gideon arrived there from the Wilderness. Steve had read about one Union prisoner who, on his release from Andersonville, discovered that the Union Army had listed him as a deserter. That probably happened more than once.

Late in the war, Confederate forces in some areas were being told to destroy records. And record keeping at this point was the least of their worries. Remarkable, Steve decided, that there is a record of so many of those who had the misfortune to be occupants of Andersonville.

So, Gideon Glenn left Andersonville alive! Where did he go?

CHAPTER 11

From "Greenhorn" to "C. W. Buff":

"Thanks for suggesting the Andersonville prison records. Turns out my man was listed! And it appears he walked out alive! But when, and to where, there's no record. I've learned that they started moving prisoners out of there in wholesale numbers in late 1864. Maybe because of the conditions. Any thoughts as to where to go from here?"

From "C. W. Buff" to "Greenhorn":

"Yes, the medics had urged moving prisoners out of Andersonville. But what probably tipped the scales was when they heard in early September of '64 that Sherman had captured Atlanta and was starting southward. He might be on a collision course with the place, which could free 30,000 Union soldiers, some of them still capable of fighting.

"You could leave if you were able to walk. Thousands were shipped to Savannah, and likewise Charleston, and more to a stockade at Florence, South Carolina. The prisoners in Savannah ended up scattered about.

As for Charleston – most of them wound up at Florence. That's your target -- Florence. Sorry, I don't believe many of the Florence records survived the war."

It took little time for Steve to confirm what "Buff" had to say about the records at Florence. No lists of survivors. There was a list of some of those who had died there, about 1,800 confirmed names. But they estimated that the deaths totaled about 3,000.

Steve reached the conclusion that Florence was little improvement over Andersonville. It was a similar design – upright timbers sunk into the ground surrounding an area of maybe 30 acres, some of it swampy and, like Andersonville, with a stream running through the center of it.

From September, 1864, through the following February, 15,000 or more Union soldiers inhabited the place. And any advantages to being at Florence as opposed to Andersonville were quickly negated by the fact that many of the men were in deplorable condition by the time they had reached the stockade.

The prisoners had just survived a brutal summer exposed to the Georgia sun. Now they were facing the cold and wet winter months, most of the men with little in the way of clothes or blankets.

Why did the Confederacy pick Florence? Steve noted it was an important railroad junction. But the area was sparsely populated. It must have been a shock to the village when 15,000 Union prisoners began limping in. Limping for sure –

those who made the trip from Andersonville to Florence in a cross-country forced march.

Steve was disappointed that he didn't find Gideon's name but at the same time relieved that he wasn't on the short list of those who had perished at the Florence Stockade.

Looking at the list, Steve remembered something "C. W. Buff" had told him. In an earlier message he had said, "When you're looking for a man, look for his regiment. Through thick or thin, the men stuck with their unit. And when something caused a soldier to be dislocated, such as being taken prisoner, he always looked for his comrades. So look for the regiment. That can put you on the right track."

Steve "Googled" the Oneida County Historical Society, which was located in Utica, New York, and found their phone number. Did they have a list of those who served in the 146th Regiment, New York State Volunteers? It took two phone calls to learn that they did not. But they thought the main library in Oneida did have such a list. It had been painstakingly put together some years after the Civil War from company muster rolls.

The library had it. And it was available for copying. A list of over a thousand names of those who had served in the 146th. Steve arranged for a high school student named Rodney to copy the list and mail to him. This for $50 plus the cost of copying and mailing. Was this an adequate reimbursement? He gathered after a couple of calls to Rodney that it was.

Originally, Steve had requested a list only of those in Company F of the 146th Regiment.

But the list, he found, was alphabetical by name, the only breakdown having to do with whether a soldier had enlisted in the fall of 1862 as one of the "Original" members of the regiment, or whether he had enlisted at a later date.

The list, on its arrival, was fairly quick to provide clues. The first name on the list furnished a glance at the major ill fortune to befall so many in the regiment:

AGNE, FREDERICK J. – Age 21 years. Enlisted. August 27, 1862, at Utica, to serve three years; mustered in as private, Co. F, October 10, 1862; promoted corporal, no date. Killed in action, May 5, 1864, at the Wilderness, Va.

Moving through the names Steve soon found the clue he was looking for:

BROWER, LORENZO – Age 22 years. Enlisted August 29, 1862, at Lee, to serve three years; mustered in as private, Co. F, Oct. 10, 1862;captured in action, May 5, 1864, at the Wilderness, Va.; died of disease, November 26, 1864, at Florence, S.C.

So, here were two members of Gideon's company who had met ill fortune at the Wilderness. And one of them had reached the Florence stockade. And there were more names of men who had "died of disease at Florence, S. C.", all of them late in 1864. Then he found a listing that might provide another piece of the puzzle:

GOFF, JOHN W. – Age 19 years. Enlisted August 30, 1862, at Augusta, to serve three years; mustered in as private, Co. G, October 10, 1862; promoted sergeant, no date; captured in action, May 5, 1864, at the Wilderness, Va.; paroled, March 2, 1865, at Wilmington, N. C.; mustered out, July 22, 1865.

Had this man by any chance gone from the Wilderness to Andersonville to the Florence Stockade to Wilmington, North Carolina? Was this the route taken by others in the regiment who were captured at the Wilderness? Perhaps including Gideon Glenn?

Steve went to the internet and clicked on Wilmington. Two substantial sources of information, the Cape Fear Museum and the New Hanover County Public Library in Wilmington, had much to say about the Civil War. But from the titles the subject matter appeared to be all about the Confederacy. And no mention of any Union prisoners having been there.

What about Fort Fisher? The port of Wilmington, Steve learned, was considered "the lifeline of the Confederacy" for much of the war, and the Confederate-held fort overlooked the Atlantic and the Cape Fear River that passed Wilmington on its way to the sea. Thanks to the fort, Union ships were unable to prevent vital supplies from reaching Wilmington, and from there via railroad to Lee's forces in Virginia.

It was the last Confederate fort not taken by Union forces, protecting the only port still open to blockade runners. It fell in mid-January of 1865, a huge blow to the Confederacy. And, Steve realized, the fort was just about the last place they would be holding Union prisoners. The Rebels at the fort had all they could handle keeping the Federal gunboats at bay.

No mention anywhere of Union prisoners in Wilmington. But Steve had now found names of several members of the regiment who had been "paroled" there, all in 1865. He decided to consult with "C. W. Buff":

"Have traced several members of my ancestor's regiment from the Wilderness to Wilmington, N.C. Possibly by way of Florence. But why Wilmington? I find no Confederate prison there. And no mention of any Union men having been in Wilmington. Any ideas?"

A rapid reply was forcoming from "C. W. Buff":

"Union prisoners probably left the Florence stockade for the same reason they departed Andersonville. Sherman. He was heading north through Georgia, so it was decided to move the prisoners to North Carolina. They sent all able-bodied prisoners to Greensboro and sick and wounded prisoners to Wilmington. The last of the prisoners left the stockade in February of 1865. By that time, though, Wilmington was in Union hands. Fort Fisher had fallen in January. (I looked it up.)"

C. W. Buff

Steve had hardly digested this information when he received another message from his Confederate pen pal:

"Why don't you come down here for a look-see? I could introduce you to a couple of folks who might be of help. My name is Barney Pollard, and I live in Myrtle Beach, South Carolina, and it's just a hop, skip and a jump up the coast to Wilmington. Let me know if you're interested."

C. W. Buff

CHAPTER 12

Steve viewed the scene from his ocean-front room in North Myrtle Beach. What a great spot for a land-lubber! He had visited the ocean infrequently in his lifetime. It was late afternoon, almost time to meet Barney Pollard.

He made the drive in short order, entered Thoroughbred's, on Restaurant Row in North Myrtle Beach, walked up to the two girls behind the desk, and said, "Barney Pollard?"

He was escorted to a table where sat a man who could easily fit the picture Steve had in his mind of "C. W. Buff." He was maybe just a little older than Steve would have guessed. Before Steve could say anything, Barney jumped up and said, "Steve Glenn, I betcha!"

Steve smiled, and extended his hand. "I'm glad to finally meet the man who seems to have read most everything written about the Civil War."

"That's not true. You know, they say that for each day since Grant and Lee met at Appomattox there has been another book published on the Civil War. It remains a hot subject. How about a drink?"

"I wouldn't mind a martini on the rocks."

Barney glanced around for a waiter. "Good. You strike me as an easy-going guy, from the sound of your telephone messages. E-mail, too."

"E-mail? I didn't know e-mail messages made sounds."

"Oh, sure they do. If you listen to the tone of a few e-mails, you can pick it up. So, you're able to spend some time down here tracking your mystery man. Are you very familiar with our part of the world?"

"I've vacationed more than once in Florida," Steve said. "But I suppose I flew right over this nice spot. I would say I have yet to soak up much of the culture of the Deep South."

Barney gave a snort. "You'd better not soak up too much of our culture all at once. It's not fat-free. 'Culture' down here means deep fried. Like fried okra. Deep-fat dishes were invented in the South."

"Like hush-puppies?"

"A classic example. Around here they're so good you could make a meal out of them. That may be why the South lost the war. Too weak from clogged arteries stuffed with saturated fats. The soldiers had no choice but to surrender."

Steve smiled. "Strange. I don't remember anything about saturated fats in Longstreet's memoirs. Anyway, I love what little I've seen of this area. Love at first sight."

"We've got a lot going here. Did you know there are more than 120 golf courses in the Myrtle Beach area? And there's a bit of history to the place, too. The first English colonists arrived here in 1730. Don't know when they built the first golf course. Did you bring your clubs?"

"I didn't inherit any golfing genes. But I'm not going to run out of things to do here, even without a tee time." Steve looked around at the growing crowd of patrons. "How did you happen to wind up in this golfer's paradise?"

"Well, it goes back a ways. After I got out of Clemson with an engineering degree I found myself peddling specialty lubricants – techical service work, really. Textile mills. And in the textile industry this area is where the action is. The work was habit forming, I guess. Stayed with it until I retired."

Barney looked away. "My long-suffering wife was anxiously awaiting retirement days. She'd grown tired of all the travel time I put in on the job, and had big plans. And then she came down with cancer and died shortly after I left the workplace. We only got a couple of retirement trips in. You married?"

"Divorced. My wife and I couldn't find the time to be married. Or so it seems, looking back on it."

"Too bad. I sure missed Marge those first few months after she was gone. Still do, but now I'm back to where the time just disappears. Right now I'm working on a speech for a luncheon club on Jeb Stuart's life and times. And a couple of days ago I led a discussion at a Civil War Roundtable on the subject of Guerilla Warfare. Civil War history keeps me hopping."

"Guerilla warfare? I believe there was a bit of that in my home state. Reminds me of a story about Mark Twain and how folks thought he had deserted the Confederate army when he went west."

"Mark Twain? Was he involved in the guerilla movement?"

"Well, he may have come close. They say he briefly joined a rag-tag outfit of volunteers before he apparently thought better of it. He later wrote about it and said the group was 'ready to fight on either side.'"

Barney laughed. "Well, those rag-tag outfits were no joke. There were plenty of them, and they caused much death and destruction. People think they were a big help to the Confederate cause, but in fact, most guerilla activity backfired. Managed to do more harm than good for the people of the South."

"Oh? How did that happen?"

"Union troops had a certain respect for Confederate forces, but they had no use for guerillas. They didn't view them as soldiers. Saw them as outlaws. Which they were. Or hoodlums."

"Troops resented their masquerading as soldiers, I suppose," Steve said.

"Yeah. And when a Union soldier was ambushed by a guerilla band, his comrades were eager to retaliate. They'd take their anger out on the people who lived in that area, often destroying everything in their path. That added up to a lot of damage."

Barney prepared to attack his filet. "So, I mentioned that friend of mine who might be of help to you in your search. His name is Frank Dillard, and he's going to be in town tomorrow. He has his home here, but he's gone a lot. I've set it up for the three of us to have lunch, if that's okay."

"I'm looking forward to it. By the way, what does Frank do?"

"Frank heads up a publishing firm called Dillard News. He owns a few newspapers and some radio property. Frank and I have been friends forever. Maybe you've heard of Dillard News."

"Yes, I'm familiar with them. They have some good properties up and down the East coast, don't they?"

"Well, most of their business is right here in the Carolinas. All healthy, I understand. Just like him. We've been friends forever.

Barney looked up from his dessert. "Incidentally, Frank's not out there re-fighting the Civil War like I am. What he brings to the party – some of his people are heavy on research. And they know the territory."

CHAPTER 13

They met the next noon at The Sea Captains House, an oceanfront restaurant on Ocean Boulevard. Barney and Frank Dillard had much to talk about, but it wasn't long before Frank peeked at the lunch menu, then dropped it and glanced over his reading glasses at Steve.

"Barney tells me you're searching for a lost ancestor," he said, "and I think this is as good a place as any to start."

Steve smiled. "I quite agree. You and Barney, I see, are men of good taste. Actually, I'm searching for anything on my great-grandfather, who disappeared during the Civil War. Captured in the Battle of the Wilderness, and the trail ended there. Until recently, that is. I just the other day learned that he was one of the ones who wound up in Andersonville, and the prison records indicate he left there alive."

Barney chimed in. "There's reason to believe he may have found his way into this area, possibly reaching Wilmington. At least, some members of his regiment did. Paroled at Wilmington near the end of the war. We thought maybe your research people could uncover something, for instance, about Union soldiers who made it as far as Wilmington but no farther.

Their names. Maybe they were buried in that area. Steve can't find anything in the records he's uncovered."

"No, as a matter of fact, information from local sources I've encountered, the Union often isn't even mentioned," Steve said. "At Florence, for instance, there's a memorial in honor of the Confederate guards who served at the stockade, but not one mention of the thousands of Union prisoners who were held there."

"Yeah, that's always a sticky wicket," Barney said. "The people who put up a memorial want to remember the boys on their side. That's what all the home folks want. They're kind of uncomfortable talking about the other side. Some of those boys starved to death while they were "visitors" in their town. You gotta be a helluva politician to come up with the right words about something like that."

Frank nodded. "Then we're all agreed with Barney's 'sticky wicket,' right? But Steve, you've got to remember the area you're talking about is dotted with graves from that era – some graves well identified, some graves of unknown soldiers and who knows how many *unknown* graves of unknown soldiers. But I'll ask our folks to see what they can find."

With that, Frank jotted a note on a pad and placed it in his pocket. "I'm still amused at how you and Barney got together," he said. "Or, should I say you and 'C. W. Buff'?"

"I'd vote for either one," Steve said. "Hearing from 'C. W. Buff' has been a joy. And educational, too."

"I can see how it would be," Frank said. "Barney's learned a lot about the so-called late unpleasantness. He's still investigating – looking for that winning formula that would have brought victory to the South."

"Well, I may have found it," Barney said. "I know a guy who claims the South would have won if they'd had more mules."

"An interesting thought," Frank said. "Maybe this area should have more statues of mules and fewer of generals on horseback. So, what are you and Steve going to do next?"

"Well, I plan to show Steve some of the sights," Barney said. "I think he likes this area."

"What's not to like?" Frank said. "Other than the traffic. Steve, what do you do when you're not searching for lost relatives?"

"Advertising, most recently," Steve said. "But I've also had some enjoyable years on the news side of the fence."

Barney shook his head. "Oh man, I'm surrounded by newshounds."

Frank laughed. "Barney, you don't seem to appreciate the importance of a free press in your way of life. I'll bet you agree with the pundit who said, 'The most important service rendered by the press is educating people to approach printed matter with distrust.'"

"The quote I remember was what Sherman had to say on the subject."

"What was that?"

He said, 'If all the newsmen were taken out and shot, there'd be news from hell by breakfast.'"

Frank reached for the check. "Barney, let me toss in this quotation – from a wise, old politician of years gone by – 'Never ever argue with somebody who buys ink by the barrel.'"

CHAPTER 14

Steve took a last look at the seaside view from his motel room and headed for the elevator. He was on his way up the coast to Wilmington, in North Carolina, with some notes from Barney as to what Frank Dillard's researchers had found.

It wasn't much. They had turned up no news stories of that era that even mentioned Union prisoners. A wealth of information about the war, and many interesting stories about Confederate soldiers' adventures and misfortunes. But no mention of prisoners having been transported to a stockade, or stories about escaped prisoners in the Wilmington area, or about local folks having seen prisoners.

But in scanning the files, someone had found a tiny story of more modern vintage about a family that had discovered a diary belonging to a Union soldier. Someone in Holly Ridge, North Carolina, north of Wilmington. They had found it while they were going through some old papers in their home dating back some generations.

The soldier apparently had seen a vast amount of action, including Gettysburg, and had finally wound up in Andersonville following his capture at the Wilderness. The soldier's name was Henry Miller, and the strange thing, according to Barney, the folks who found the diary had no idea who Miller was, or why the diary wound up in their belongings. In Barney's words, "According to the news story, they're good southerners. No Yankee ties, and at least two ancestors who were Confederates."

The story had also mentioned work being done to transcribe the contents of the diary. Not easy. The pages were brittle. The diary and transcription were going to be turned over to a museum or library in the area for public viewing. Barney had suggested Steve try the Cape Fear Museum in Wilmington.

Steve had checked an internet site before leaving Myrtle Beach. The Cape Fear Museum, he noted, was the oldest museum in North Carolina, founded in the Nineteenth Century by the Daughters of the Confederacy.

The area's history dated back to pre-Colonial times, Steve learned, with the name Cape Fear playing a prominent role. He found one mention of a voyage by a British explorer who referred to a treacherous sandbar at the mouth of the river extending through the area to the sea as "The Cape of Fear." The river being known today as the Cape Fear River.

This would be an interesting area to explore, Steve figured, whether by land or sea. He headed down Market Street in Wilmington toward the Cape Fear Museum.

Steve moved past a group of happy school kids crowded around an exhibit of "The Lower Cape Fear." They were obviously fascinated by the model sailing ships of yesteryear navigating the channel flowing by downtown Wilmington. The Cape Fear Museum was much larger than Steve had expected, modernized in recent years with add-ons to an earlier location more than tripling its size.

It was indeed spacious, complete with an auditorium and thousands of artifacts and photographs. And interesting exhibits. Steve paid particular note to a three-dimensional scene of Fort Fisher as it appeared in Civil War times. He would come back later, but it was time to move on because the Union soldier's diary wasn't there. Not a trace.

A museum employee had suggested the New Hanover County Public Library, which was already in his sights. The library had a splendid pedigree. State and local history was housed there, much of it handed down through former libraries dating back to the Cape Fear Library of 1760.

An earlier visit to the internet had brought up the library's ground rules. All research must be done in the North Carolina Room from 9 am to 8 pm. Copy machines available for materials not too brittle. Pencils preferred to pens. "Write or call first."

It was a short drive to the main library in downtown Wilmington. And, as expected, to a treasure-trove of information about Civil War days. But it appeared to be a dry hole as far as uncovering any information about a Union soldier named Henry Miller, or a Union prisoner in North Carolina, or a Civil War diary belonging to Miller. Regardless of the approach, no information surfaced that didn't pertain to Confederate forces.

No information, that is, until the librarian at a nearby counter suggested Steve try the library's Genealogy room. There, in the section cataloged under the letter "N," as in New Haven County, with mention of the folks in Holly Ridge who found it, was a transcript of the diary he was seeking. A partial transcript, that is, of the pages that were legible. And a reference to the fact that the original pages were too brittle for viewing. And the title read, "Diary of Henry Miller, Private, Company G, 146th Regiment, New York Volunteers." The elusive "Fifth Oneida!"

Steve went to a table and, with some impatience, started leafing through the transcript. It seemed Henry Miller had been everywhere. The diary entries dated back to the fall of 1862 in his first days in camp at Rome, New York.

The first action described in the diary was in mid-December, 1862, in Virginia, at the Battle of Fredericksburg, although according to Miller his regiment was not in the line of fire when "so many lives were lost storming the Heights." The regiment, he said, was most fortunate not to be among those called to advance on the Confederate positions. Most of their time was spent in rear guard action before the units were finally withdrawn from the area.

A dreary winter followed the Fredericksburg campaign at an encampment on the Rappahannock River, and the diary made occasional references to the camp routine – "drilling, drilling and more drilling," and illness (the camp was known as "Camp Dysentery"). And cold, and lack of creature comforts, and occasional light-hearted moments but more often than not, boredom.

Then in April of '63 the diary entries picked up as rumors abounded that they were about to march, this time the army under the command of "Fighting Joe" Hooker, who had replaced Burnside following the Union disaster at Fredericksburg.

It was the start of the Chancellorsville campaign, where the 146th received its first full-blown baptism of fire, as Steve had noted earlier in a brief history of the regiment. The diary reported "several casualties in the regiment." The diary also described their advance on Chancellorsville "on a night in which shells tore through the forest, and horses and mules ran in all directions, some pulling clattering wagons as troops advanced and others retreated in a moon-lit scene of utmost confusion."

Another disastrous campaign. Steve moved on in 1863 to late June and the regiment's hurried march north toward Gettysburg before it occurred to him he was running short of library time. He could come back to that. Maybe he could copy the transcript. But in the meantime, what happened to Private Miller? Steve leafed through the transcript until he came to some diary entries about "total chaos" at the Wilderness, then a time gap in the diary and then a mention of his capture. And then a few entries at Andersonville. Not many. The last entry in September, 1864. And then, a few pages later, some entries from Florence, South Carolina. Private Miller had indeed made it to the Florence Stockade!

Steve turned to the last few pages of the transcript, the entries dated in the early days of 1865. The prisoners, and guards, were on the move:

February 9, 1865

Not that the Florence Stockade was a great place to visit, but we all would vote to go back there if we could. We can't long endure this march, if you can call it that. Some of our men can scarcely crawl. The guards seem sympathetic, as they, too, are hungry, cold and tired, although they don't begin to resemble our pathetic bunch.

Where were they going? Steve turned to the next entry, and learned a bit more about their ordeal.

February 12, 1865

For a dollar, Confederate, bought a supply of gubers from a guard, and now that I've got them what do I do? I've lost three or four teeth. Hard food's a chore. But I'll try. I could eat a sow's ear. The nights are terrible. Very cold. But it doesn't discourage the lice.

The next item shed a little more light on the whereabouts of these unfortunates.

February 14, 1865

They say we're in North Carolina now and heading for Wilmington, which is near the Coast. Seem to be going easterly. Countryside isn't as rugged. But every mile is a mile too many. We need a rest. And my kingdom for a large helping of corn bread and ham, or whatever else might be available in this country.

The next entry brought Steve up with a start.

February 17, 1865

People we meet stare at us with great curiosity, but are quick to look away if we make eye contact. One of them told the guards that an old negro had told him "Lincoln Men" had taken over Wilmington! The guards were very upset. We've made a left turn. Away from Wilmington. Don't know where we're going but we'd better get there soon. The fevers are going to claim some of us. Don't think Gideon will last much longer.

Gideon? Was it a coincidence? Gideon was a common name in those days, Gideon Welles, Lincoln's secretary of the navy, for instance. Steve hurried on to the next entry.

February 20, 1865

We said farewell to Gideon Glenn this morning. Left him behind on property belonging to a Mr. Stearns, close to a family burial ground on his place. The guards asked permission to leave him, and we asked if, on Gideon's passing, he could be buried in that cemetery. Mr. Stearns is a born Confederate but he was much moved by Gideon's plight and seemed touched by our situation as well. I hope he puts a marker on the grave. He said he would. We're off shortly to a hamlet up the road called Castle Hayne. Hope there's something there in the way of grub.

CHAPTER 15

Steve had pinpointed two Stearns families in the Castle Hayne area and was pulling up in front of the first of the two. Off route 117, about ten miles north of Wilmington. Not very promising. A small, unpretentious house inside the city limits of Castle Hayne. Not a large piece of property and there was certainly no place for a family burial ground.

Steve rang the bell and was greeted by Wilbur M. Stearns, a pleasant man. Steve got to the point as quickly as he could – a genealogy mission, attempting to find the grave of an ancestor who he believes may have been buried in a family burial ground in the area, on property belonging to a Mr. Stearns.

A smiling Wilbur Stearns said there was "no such animal" in his family. No, he and his wife had never lived in the country. Did he have any ancestors who were around here during the Civil War? No, his father was the first to settle in the Castle Hayne area. "He was in a war, though – World War II." Did Wilbur Stearns know the family of Robert Wren Stearns, some distance northwest of here? No, but he was aware of them. "We got some of their mail one time."

The home of Robert Wren Stearns turned out to be a farm house on what appeared to be considerable acreage. Urban sprawl had not yet approached this part of the world. Steve drove up the drive to a parking area to the left of the house, where he was greeted by two big, noisy dogs. Tails wagging. Noisy but happy. It was the only cordial reception Steve was to receive.

Robert Stearns was a cantankerous old man who viewed Steve with suspicion if not downright hostility. Steve's questioning was cut short. He left without even learning whether there was a Mrs. Stearns he could talk to, and he wished he had called first.

Maybe he would have reached someone easier to approach.

Steve decided to go into town to see if he couldn't search out a relative. Perhaps a son or daughter. He had no trouble finding someone who knew Robert Wren Stearns. But had problems finding out much about the family. There was a Mrs. Stearns, all right, one shopkeeper said, but there was only one "kid" to his knowledge, and he lived "out west somewhere."

Steve wasn't sure he wanted to approach Mrs. Stearns as yet. He decided to look further, and entered a nearby coffee shop. The waitress who brought his coffee said, yes, she was familiar with Robert Stearns but knew nothing about the family. "But Sheila probably would. She knows everybody."

Sheila, the other waitress on duty, finally arrived at Steve's table. "You're looking for the Stearns place?"

"I'm familiar with their location," Steve said. "I'm wondering if there is someone in the Stearns family that I could talk to."

Sheila put a coffee carafe back on the burner and returned to the table." Mr. Stearns lives at the family place."

Steve smiled. "Someone other than Mr. Stearns, if possible. He seems a little difficult to talk to."

"Well, I went to school with a niece, lives in Wilmington now. The niece is named Linda Stearns. Do you have business with them, or something?"

"Not business," Steve said. "I'm on a genealogy mission. The Stearns family and my family seem to have something in common, and I'd like to talk to her about it. Could you by any chance supply me her address or phone number?"

"No, she just recently moved to Wilmington," Sheila said. "Not sure where she moved to, but she's working for an insurance company there."

"Linda Stearns." Steve wrote it down. "Still carrying the Stearns name."

"Yeah, she's not married. I guess she and her boyfriend were pretty close to it. But he was in the aerial spray business and one day he clipped the power lines. Let me ask someone what's the name of that insurance outfit."

CHAPTER 16

Steve punched in the number of the insurance agency in Wilmington and was mildly surprised when a live voice responded. Not a menu of choices as so often happens. He asked for Linda Stearns and was somewhat relieved when the voice said, "One moment please." It appeared he was on the right track.

A warm voice came on the line. "Linda Stearns."

"Linda, my name is Steve Glenn, and I'm on a genealogy mission. I'm searching for a long lost relative, and I have reason to believe you can help me."

There was silence on the line, so Steve continued. "I went to see your uncle, Robert Stearns, about this, but had trouble discussing it with him. He apparently thought I was trying to sell him something."

"I don't think I understand what ..."

"Linda, let me ask you just one question. Is there a family burial ground on the acreage where Mr. Stearns lives?"

"Yes, there is. Or was. But I really don't have time to ....."

"Linda, I have found something to indicate that a relative of mine may have been buried in that plot." The line was silent and Steve hoped she was still there. "I'd like to tell you a little about the man and ask just a couple of questions. Could we meet somewhere after work? Are you familiar with the Pilot House on the waterfront?" A pause. "I understand they have good appetizers."

"I don't think you'd find anyone in Wilmington not familiar with it." She hesitated. "I gather you're not from this area."

"No, I'm from St. Louis. Back in Missouri. You might say I'm here because footsteps from the past brought me. Look, I know this may sound frivolous to you, getting so wound up in something to do with genealogy. I'm sure it's meaningless to many."

"No, no, I understand. But I think you've made a mistake. I don't believe there is anyone in that burial ground other than family."

"I have some information dating clear back to Civil War days that indicates that this indeed happened. It spells out a situation that occurred back then, and I'm sure you would be interested in it. How it came about." He paused. "Linda, I'd really like to talk to you about this. Would you prefer some place other than the Pilot House? Could we meet after you get off?"

"Well, I couldn't stay long. But, okay. I could spare a little time right after work. If that's all right. I'm off at 5. The Pilot House is fine."

It was an intriguing view for a landlubber from the Midwest, the scene from the Pilot House, and Steve was taking it all in. His table looked out on boat traffic making headway up and down the Cape Fear River. A bustling sight, fit for a commercial photographer. In St. Louis the Missouri and Mississippi Rivers didn't offer as many picture postcard views as this, Steve decided.

He wondered what it was like back in Civil War days. Possibly the "Lower Cape Fear" was even busier back then, judging from the exhibit he had viewed at the Cape Fear Museum.

He was watching a southbound trawler moving smartly along when the girl from the front desk appeared with Linda. She was a good match, Steve thought, for the pleasant voice he'd heard on the telephone.

He arose and gestured toward a seat. "Hi. Thank you for coming."

When Linda was seated, she said, "Your call certainly aroused my curiosity. But let me ask you first, how did you find me? I'm fairly new on the job in Wilmington."

Steve smiled. "I found you through your friend, Sheila, in Castle Hayne. She didn't have an address or phone number, but she had a general idea where you worked."

"Oh, I should have known. In Castle Hayne you don't need a newspaper. Just ask Sheila what's going on. So, are you on vacation?"

"I'm between jobs. A good time to be searching for a lost relative. It's my great grandfather, and as I mentioned, I have some information to the effect that he was buried in the cemetery ground on your uncle's place."

"What makes you think that?"

Steve produced a photocopy from his shirt pocket. "Here is what I found. This was mentioned in the diary of a Union soldier who was there." Steve passed the copy across the table.

Linda read the few lines dated February 20, 1865 about the arrival of an ailing Gideon Glenn "on property belonging to a Mr. Stearns," and the request that on passing he be buried "in that cemetery plot." She looked up. "Where in the world did you find this?"

"This is from the transcript of the diary," Steve said. "Those pages that were still readable. It's in the county library here. This is why I went to see your uncle. I wanted to take a look, to see if I could find the grave. By the way, in our phone call you mentioned the cemetery plot in the past tense. Isn't it still intact?"

"Oh yes, it's intact," Linda said. "But it has no modern-day occupants. I'm afraid it's been lightly maintained and seldom visited. But it's still there."

"Linda, I would be indebted to you if you could arrange for me to see it. That cemetery might answer some questions that have lingered for well over a century."

Well, I don't see why it can't be worked out," Linda said. "Tomorrow's Saturday, and I'm off. I'll call Sarah about it. My aunt. Maybe I can arrange for a visit tomorrow."

CHAPTER 17

Saturday blossomed beautifully, a good day to inspect that cemetery, or if that was not feasible, any of an unlimited choice of other activities. In a call to Linda later that morning Steve learned that the visit was off for the moment.

But all was not lost. She agreed to have lunch with him and do some sight-seeing. A relief to Steve. He had been living out of a suitcase on this solo mission for some time now and Linda, he had discovered, was more than just polite company.

Steve wondered where she stood in the normal order of things. She appeared near the top of the order when it came to any judging of "southern belles" seen on his recent journey through Dixie. Where had she been? And where was she going? She had said she had some news. What was that all about?

They took over a table at a waterfront site on the Cape Fear, overlooking Battleship Park. "It was good of you to join me today", Steve said. "It takes two to enjoy a day like this. I hope I'm not messing up some plans you had."

"No, no," Linda said. "Nothing that can't wait. Besides, I wanted to tell you what I learned from Sarah. She said she had heard a story long ago, a story handed down in the Stearns family from Civil War days, about a Yankee soldier who turned up near the family cemetery. A strange story. Something to do with my great-grandfather. It's pretty sketchy, I know, but it seems to fit with what you found in the diary."

"Has she seen the grave?"

"No, she hasn't. She only vaguely recalls the story. Said it had something to do with a 'dying Yankee' being left there, in her words. She may have heard it from Uncle Robert's grandparents. Can't recall the details. She was a young bride then, new in the area, and probably had other things on her mind."

"But your uncle didn't agree to my dropping by?"

"He wasn't feeling well, and Sarah said she didn't bring it up. I'm going to go out there tonight and talk to both of them."

She waved off an attempt at an apology from Steve. "It's no problem. So, what do you think of the Wilmington area?"

"It has a lot going for it. You have an attractive riverfront city, and you're close to an ocean as well. That's a great combination."

Steve watched a triple-decker paddlewheel boat shoving off. "Oh, and one thing that particularly interests me – the area's rich history. I could spend some time here just nosing around."

"Any particular place in mind?"

"Well, we're pretty close to Fort Fisher. The place has quite a story to tell. Also, today it should be rich in salt air and sunshine."

They turned onto a road heading south from Wilmington, just to the east of the Cape Fear River. The river, Steve noted, was beginning to take on the proportions of a sound, as it approached the Atlantic. A rather impressive body of water.

"So, you've never visited Fort Fisher," Steve said.

"No, I've seen it from a distance," Linda said. "On an excursion boat."

The exit loomed ahead for the "Fort Fisher Recreational Area." They were not a great distance from the infamous Cape Fear.

"Here stands the most important earthwork fortification in the South during the Civil War," Steve said, eyeing the sandy fortress.

"It's not as big as I expected," Linda said. "I'm surprised."

"The fort isn't impressive today because most of it's gone. It was made mainly of earth and sand, and erosion has taken its toll. I read that maybe ten percent of the fort is still here. During the war the fort grew to a huge size and protected over a mile of ocean front, they say."

Steve inspected one of the gun emplacements still there. "One of the Confederate cannons reportedly could fire 150-pound shells up to five miles. British made. It's at West Point now. It sure helped keep the Union gunboats at bay."

Linda surveyed the scene. "The South did all this to defend Wilmington?"

"Well, they weren't defending Wilmington," Steve said. "What they were defending was the shipping as it approached the Cape Fear River. They were here to help the blockade runners slip in with supplies for the Confederates."

"Coming in to Wilmington?"

"That's right. The blockade runners went to Bermuda and the Bahamas with cotton and tobacco in exchange for food and clothing. And munitions. And all those supplies they brought back went by rail from Wilmington up to the Army of Northern Virginia. Lee's army, that is."

"I would think the Union could have blocked the entrance to the Cape Fear, somehow," Linda said.

"From what I've read, the Union was successful in stopping blockade runners at most ports," Steve said. "But not here. Not until late in the war. A combination of factors. Too many lanes into the Cape Fear to protect against. And artillery fire from this fort really got their attention. Union gunboats had to keep their distance."

Following a walk on nearby Kure Beach, they headed back. It was getting late in the afternoon.

Steve turned to Linda. "Can I call you in the morning?"

"Sure. Let's assume I can work out a visit to the graveyard. I'm almost as interested in this as you are."

CHAPTER 18

Steve reached Linda's apartment at 10 Sunday morning, the appointed hour. He was glad she had agreed to ride with him. Maybe they could make a day of it. Just like Saturday. He'd enjoyed that. They started north from Wilmington on route 117.

Steve glanced at Linda. "How did you manage to get your uncle to agree to this?"

"It wasn't that difficult," Linda said. "He'll listen to me, but he doesn't hear very well when Sarah talks to him. Anyway, I convinced him that it would be a shame for someone to travel a long distance to visit the grave of a relative and be denied the opportunity." Linda smiled. "When I left there, he sounded almost as if your visiting was his idea."

"Glad it worked out. Thanks for going to bat for me."

They turned into the lengthy drive that led to the home of Robert Wren Stearns, and stopped in the parking area to the left of the house. They were greeted by the two big, noisy dogs that had approached Steve with enthusiasm on his first visit. This time they gave Steve the cold shoulder when they realized their friend, Linda, was there.

"I guess your aunt and uncle have been alerted to our arrival," Steve said.

"Oh, they've probably gone to church," Linda said. "Anyway, they have no knowledge of the gravesite. Just that rather vague story passed down about a Yankee soldier being left here." She pointed to a grove of trees some distance to the left. "The burial ground is behind that grove."

Rolling pastureland separated them from the grove. They let themselves through the gate and started in that direction. "It's my fondest hope that there's some sort of marker on that grave," Steve said.

"I'm quite sure I would have heard about that, if it existed. Sarah and Uncle Robert would surely have seen it. Or would have remembered hearing about it."

Behind the grove of trees they found the Stearns Family Cemetery, surrounded by a waist-high chain-link fence. Stepping stones led to a gate, which Steve opened.

It was a secluded spot. The grove of trees encroached on the fence line, and wild shrubbery threatened both sides of the fence. With the passage of time, vegetation had formed a cover over some of the area.

Linda surveyed the scene. "Why do you suppose your man Gideon happened to wind up here? Near Castle Hayne, of all places. Were they by any chance looking for Wilmington?"

"They were trying to avoid Wilmington, Steve said. "The Confederate guards had heard that Fort Fisher had fallen and Union troops were in Wilmington. And Sherman was in the neighborhood. He'd moved up the Carolina coast from Savannah and was routing any Confederate forces around."

"So, the North came into the Carolinas from the south?"

"That's about right. In any event, the guards with the prisoners were probably trying to reach Confederate units, and they might have to go as far north as Virginia to do it."

Steve noted there were close to a dozen ancient tombstones in the burial ground, generally clustered toward the center of the enclosure. All family members of generations past.

"I see what you mean. You said there were no modern-day occupants."

"No, this is a thing of the past, and as you can see, the place is rather lightly maintained," Linda said. "And it's seldom visited. I understand my uncle mows it occasionally."

Steve surveyed the area. "I guess somewhere near the fence is where we need to start looking."

They walked to the back of the plot. A mower could not quite reach the fenceline any more because underbrush was encroaching. Steve picked up a branch of a few feet in length and proceeded to poke at the ground cover.

"I'll go get something out of the tool shed that we can work with," Linda said.

She returned with a rake and a hoe, and they started moving along the fenceline, feeling their way. They went the length of the fence, Linda following along behind Steve. Then a second sweep, to no avail.

"Looks like this is a job for modern technology," Steve said. "Like a gasoline-powered weed whipper for starters. And maybe a once-over with a mower."

As he moved away from the fence, Steve caught himself when his foot tripped over something. He knelt to inspect it. A rock, maybe. He pried earth away from it for a better look. A gravestone? Additional excavating indicated it could be something handcrafted.

"There's something here, Linda," Steve said.

"A headstone?"

"Could be. It's shaped like it."

Presently Steve had it sufficiently cleared for a close inspection. It didn't take long. He looked up at Linda and shook his head.

"The search continues. Sorry to get your hopes up. And mine. Anyway, it's getting late. Let's break 'til tomorrow."

CHAPTER 19

Sarah placed a tall glass of iced tea in front of Steve, who was enjoying the shade in the back yard of the the Stearns place. She took a spot across from Steve and Linda at the picnic table.

"What a waste of a holiday," she said. Half of it, anyway. I'm really sorry you didn't find the grave."

"I'm only concerned that I wasted half of Linda's holiday," Steve said. "We sure came up empty, didn't we? Well, anyway, I must say the cemetery plot looks a lot better for the effort."

"It's amazing, how much better, Sarah said. "You certainly spruced it up. Robert is very happy with it."

Steve had spent most of the morning clearing the graveyard of brush around the fencelines, and mowing the grass down to size. If no other benefit, Steve thought, at least he had succeeded in thawing out Mr. Stearns, who he spotted heading in their direction.

Mr. Stearns poured a full glass of iced tea and sat next to Sarah. "So, what are you folks cookin' up?"

"Looks like we're done cookin,'" Sarah said. "We were just wondering what else Steve could do to locate that relative. It's a shame he didn't find anything."

Linda shook her head. "Steve has put so much effort into this. If only we'd found some clue. So Steve could close the book on Gideon. Where else is there to look?"

"Yeah, I'm afraid that Civil War diary was the last word," Steve said. "I guess we've exhausted our supply of clues."

Mr. Stearns turned toward Sarah. "How about those old family papers up in George's attic? Some of them are pretty ancient. May be something in there about that soldier they say was left here."

"Robert Stearns, what are you talking about?" Sarah's voice had an edge to it.

"Why, there's a whole trunkload of paperwork up there. Been there forever. There's old family letters, legal documents, stuff that nobody wanted to throw away. Oh yeah, ancient photographs, tintypes, that sort of thing."

Steve pulled out his pocket notepad. "Who, may I ask, is George?"

"And how come you know so much about what's in his attic?" Sarah added.

"He's my cousin," Robert Stearns said. "When we were kids George and I used to play at his place. That's how come I wound up pokin' about in his attic. Once when we were playin' around up there I saw it. This collection. Pretty old. Lots of letters and stuff."

"The name's George Stearns?"

"No, the name's George Durant. His mother was Freda, one of Isaac's daughters. I guess I should mention, Isaac is the 'Mr. Stearns' you encountered in that diary. He was my great grandfather."

Steve gestured toward the Stearns farm home. "Did Isaac Stearns build this house?"

"No no. The house Isaac lived in is long gone. But it's the same site, or pretty close."

"I wonder what George's attic looks like," Sarah said. "If it's anything like ours, it's a disaster. Robert won't ever let me throw anything away up there. I figure a bomb's the only sure way to clear it."

"Could be," Mr. Stearns said. "But before you throw a grenade in any attics, maybe these kids would like to go take a look. Place is about three miles northwest of here. I'll call and see what he's doing."

CHAPTER 20

Steve surveyed the scene as they entered the drive to the Durant farm home. Everything looked spic and span except for one rather tall, weathered structure with a pitched roof – a tobacco curing barn, Steve guessed.

George Durant gave the four of them a hearty welcome, and it was apparent to Steve that he and Robert Stearns were still kids at heart when the two of them got together. Seated in the rather cozy family room of the Durant home Steve noted framed photos of healthy-looking tobacco plants in the field. "Mr. Durant," he said, "I noted that tobacco barn as we were driving up. Is that still operational?"

"My name's George. And that tobacco barn's a relic. They bulk-cure tobacco now. I don't know. I could sell that timber tomorrow, or I might turn the place into a storage shed. Only problem, if you don't maintain the thing it'll quickly go from rustic to dilapidated, real quick."

"How's the tobacco business?"

"You mean raising tobacco? I'm done with it. Hardly anyone around here raises tobacco any more. It's a thing of the past, same as that tobacco barn."

"Is demand dropping?"

"Oh no. It's going up in some countries. But supply is skyrocketing. Tobacco cultivation has gone world-wide, where labor's cheap. And growers here have no price support any more. It was bound to happen."

"But there are other crops that are adapted to this area," Robert Stearns remarked.

"Oh sure," George said. "There's cotton, corn and truck crops, that sort of thing. But there's not near as much joy at harvest time as there was with brightleaf tobacco."

"I suppose this has really changed farming around here," Steve said.

George Durant chuckled. "Well, let me put it this way. For a century or so, tobacco paid the bills. And it built roads and schools. Hell, in North Carolina it's even built cities. It goes clear back to the Civil War."

"The Civil War?" Steve said. "How did the Civil War get involved?"

"Well, that's when tobacco really took over. It was growing in popularity, and suddenly it got a blessing from the government. Both governments, I should say. Both Union and Confederate troops started getting regular rations of tobacco, and they took a liking to the brightleaf from around here. Probably all our ancestors started puffing away back then. Puffing when they weren't chewing."

"That's better than fighting," Robert Stearns said. He scooped some cashews off a dish on the coffee table. "George, I told Steve our ancestors preferred to make love, not war. So, not much to report, as far as the Civil War is concerned.

George Durant laughed. "Guess that's partially true, far as the Stearns family is concerned. I've researched both families a little bit. Actually, your grandfather Benjamin was a little too young to fight. And so was Samuel." He glanced toward Linda. "Samuel was Linda's great-grandfather. But that doesn't rule out the Durants. I had two ancestors fought with the Rebs."

Robert Stearns snorted. "Okay, tell us about 'em."

"Not much to tell. They both died while they were in camp for the winter."

"They died of boredom?"

"Robert, that's not very nice," Sarah said. "But, I wonder, why in the world did the soldiers spend a whole winter in camp? I'd think they would have preferred to keep fighting and get it over with."

"The answer to that, I guess, is mud," George Durant said.

Robert Stearns looked up. "Did you say 'mud'?"

"Yep. It's always been a great defense against a military attack. In the Civil War, when the weather got bad heavy artillery bogged down. Narrow wheels. Cut the roads to ribbons, and sometimes even the mules couldn't budge an artillery piece."

"So, they set up a winter camp?"

"Right, and then sickness started. Most of the soldiers were youngsters who had not been away from home before, and they'd never been exposed to the diseases that would invade a camp. Oftentimes childhood diseases. Especially in winter. Also the men were exposed to the elements – rain, snow and cold -- and that didn't help."

"They didn't know much about sanitation, either," Steve added. "In an account I read about my great grandfather's regiment they called their winter quarters, 'Camp Dysentery.'" Steve pulled out his notepad. "So Isaac Stearns had two boys?"

"Right. Two sons and two daughters."

Robert Stearns reached for some more cashews. "George, I told these kids you had a trunk full of old correspondence and such up in your attic, family tree stuff and all. Don't know why we don't have anything like that in our place. Guess we were better at throwing things away."

"That's not the entire story," George Durant said. "That trunk was mainly Freda's doing." He looked at Steve. "She was my grandmother. As I understand it, before they tore down the old house that Isaac Stearns built, Freda went over there and rescued lots of memorabilia. Family stuff mostly.

Including anything left behind by Becky. That's her sister. I believe Becky got married and moved west. Don't know what you'll find, but you're welcome to go up there and have a look."

CHAPTER 21

It was apparent that the attic in the Durant house had long been a storehouse for both treasure and trash. Much like Sarah's description of the Stearns attic. Steve had uncovered some dusty Christmas decorations, a baby carriage, an ancient chiffonier filled with old dresses and some newspapers, one with a huge banner headline announcing that the "Japs" had bombed Pearl Harbor.

There were boxes of odds and ends, also suitcases stuffed with clothes. And magazines of a different era. Steve proceeded to move the magazines aside. "I think this place contains just about every edition of the 'Saturday Evening Post' ever printed," he said.

Several feet away Linda trained her flashlight on an area not exposed to the attic light. "Steve, I think there's a trunk back in here. I can see a corner of it, but there's boxes in the way."

Once Steve got the area cleared the trunk took center stage. "I'll bet this baby was a beauty in its day," Steve said. "All it needs is a little cleaning and polishing. Let me pull it out under the light and see what we've got."

With some effort Steve moved the trunk. He lifted the clasp. The lid opened without resistance and they were viewing what appeared to be the letters of several lifetimes dating back to a much different era, a letter-writing age. The trunk's contents seemed in good condition.

Steve stifled a sneeze. "It's not quite like volcanic ash, but that dust gets your attention."

"Why don't we sort through some of the letters in here first," Linda said. "We could clear off that table over by the stairs and see if there's any rhyme or reason here."

"You'll have to help me on this," Steve said. "I don't know the names of the players, not too many, anyway." He began lifting items from the trunk, many of the letters still in their envelopes, for stacking on the table.

The name on one of the envelopes caught Steve's eye. "Here's one addressed to Becky Stearns. Wasn't she one of the daughters of Isaac Stearns?"

"Yes, let me see that. Hmmm, this is from Becky's older sister, Freda. She seems to be working in a hospital in Portsmouth, Virginia. My word, this was written in 1864!" And look at this postmark! I didn't know they had postmarks clear back in Civil War times."

"Oh, postmarks go all the way back to Colonial days in this country. Idea borrowed from Great Britain, I suppose. I think they used postmarks quite a long time before stamps hit the scene."

Steve delved deeper into the stack. "Here's another letter to Becky. And here's a couple to Freda. Let's see. Yes, Becky wrote these. And here's a deed for some property Mr. Stearns bought." Steve picked up a newspaper clipping that was buried in the stack. "There's a wealth of history here. You'll be interested in this."

"Wait! Steve, you've got to read this." Linda reached over and handed a letter to Steve. The letter brought Steve up with a start. It was addressed to:

Mr. Gideon Glenn, Esq.

Dear Mr. Glenn:

Your letter of the 2th instant, addressed to Fanny Glenn, came to hand yesterday. We were quite surprised to learn that you are still alive, having assumed long ago that you had passed on during the Late Unpleasantness.

In regard to Fanny Glenn, it falls to my unhappy lot to inform you that Fanny has gone on to her reward, after some weeks of suffering the ill effects of typhoid fever. As for her son, Judd, he is now a member of the household of Fanny's sister, Evelyn, and I am pleased to report that Judd is very much at home there with Evelyn's two children. You may rest assured that he will continue to receive the best of care.

It must always be remembered that it is through the amazing mercy of God that we are alive and well. Trusting that you are recovering well from the travails of your wartime experiences, I remain,

Yours Most Sincerely

Elias McIntosh

Steve looked at Linda. "I am slightly stunned," he said. "Gideon survived the war? Where did he go? Not back to New York, apparently."

"What a strange letter," Linda said. "Who is Elias McIntosh?"

"I assume that was Gideon's father-in-law. McIntosh was Fanny Glenn's maiden name."

Linda shook her head. It sounds almost as though his father-in-law was inviting him not to come back."

"Well, I don't think there was any love lost between those two, from what I've heard," Steve said. "Let's see. The date on this letter is hard to read, but I think it's dated May something, 1865. Hmmm. You suppose they took Gideon to a hospital?"

"Steve, this will answer a lot of your questions." Linda handed him another of the letters from the stack. It was from Becky to Freda, and it was about Gideon. Steve could easily read Becky's flowing handwriting.

It was dated March 30/65:

"Further on the visitor who is changing our lives, we're not supposed to be doing this, but the war seems almost over and I no longer care. His name is Gideon. Father was opposed at first to the idea of moving him into the house. Now father spends time with him every day.

"Gideon is improving rapidly, and we are now taking short walks together outside. I must say he is a most unusual man. A fine person, really. And to think that not too long ago father was almost certain he was going to die, and I was praying for him.

"We have a Negro woman doing much of the work, and she is very good. Father pays her and she has sleeping quarters here. I think she might be somebody's slave but she says she is a freed woman, and the way things are going I don't believe it matters. Soldiers have quit coming around looking for runaways. Or deserters either, for that matter. It is quite chaotic here.

"I can't think of anything else to mention. Our guest seems to be occupying my thoughts. More later."

Becky

Steve put the letter down. "I wonder ….."

"Steve," Linda interrupted, "It's getting late and I've got to go to work tomorrow Let's just package all these letters and I'll see if my uncle won't let us borrow them. You've had enough surprises for one day."

CHAPTER 22

The following Saturday noon found Sarah Stearns busily preparing sandwiches and salad for the folks in the den at the Stearns home – husband Robert, George Durant, Linda, and Steve Glenn, who was soon to depart the area.

Mr. Durant was pouring over one of the letters Steve had culled from the Durant collection. "Listen to this one, Robert. It's from Becky to Freda, and it's dated April 3, 1869:

'This is my first letter to you since I wrote about our preparations for heading west across the state of Iowa. We are now in a bustling little town called Sioux City. It is on the Missouri River, which sees a lot of traffic from southward to here. Gideon is very busy at a saddlery, and there is always much to be done. The business is close to a number of cattle pens on the Floyd River, which flows into the Missouri.

'We are doing well, and I would just as soon stay here and make this our permanent home. But Gideon, as you know, wants to move on as soon as we can. He has his eyes on land to the north of here. Not yet, though. It is not safe to venture north at the moment because of Indian problems.'

The letter goes on to talk about their place in Sioux City. And on the envelope, by the way, is the name, 'Becky Glenn.'"

"So, they moved to Iowa," Robert Stearns said. "Where did you say they got married?"

"I didn't say," George Durant replied.

Steve laughed. "Well, 'where and when' is a little bit up in the air, but I think I can find that out. Mr. Durant, why don't you read that next letter?"

"Oh yeah, Robert. Listen to this – from Becky to Freda, dated May, 1872, and now they're farming:

'This is my first letter from our new location in northwest Iowa. It is beautiful country, really, but so different from home. Fewer trees and fewer people.

Much distance between what few settlements exist, but everyone is friendly and helpful. We are 20 to 30 miles from the western border of Iowa, and west of that is Dakota territory.

'Gideon says it's the best farmland he's ever seen. We are homesteading 160 acres, and the land will be totally ours in five years. But so much work to do! Meanwhile, though, I am enjoying life here with Gideon. It always stays rather pleasant in the summertime, and I love the rolling landscape and the lush grain fields.

'At the moment, Gideon is dragging timber to the site where he will build our new home. This is prairie country and away from rivers timber is limited. Gideon has bought the wood from a family living near the water.

'We are temporarily staying in a sod house, and I must say it is fairly comfortable. It actually feels warmer in cold weather than in a log or frame home. Just the same, I will be looking forward to the day when Gideon finishes our new home.'

And the letter goes on to ask some questions of Freda."

"George, you need to clean up your attic more often," Robert Stearns said. "Steve, you have any idea where this farm is located?"

"Only that it's in Sioux County, Iowa. Postmarks on the letters weren't any help, but I'm quite sure that's the county from the geographical description of the farm property. Also from Becky's mention of the distance south to Sioux City, which incidentally is not in Sioux County."

"Steve is going back there to see what he can find out," Linda said.

Mr. Durant looked puzzled. "Going back there? Steve, can't you call someone for information?"

Steve shook his head. "I've tried that. Called the county recorder's office, also tried to access county records on the web, also checked some genealogy sites. The county recorder's office says I can trace property ownership back as far as 1870 in their files. They also have birth, marriage and death records dating back that far."

"Birth records? Your ancestor was born in New York, wasn't he?"

"Yes, but maybe his name appears in the Iowa records in connection with the birth of an offspring."

"You say the records have the name of the original owner of the property?"

"Yes, they said that in most cases you should be able to find the original owner. But they went on to say that it depends to some extent on when the deed was recorded. I suppose some people are slow getting around to it. Anyway, it looks like it's time for more legwork."

"Sioux County Iowa!" George Durant said. "That's a long way from the Radio City Music Hall. Do you need safari gear for that trip?"

"Oh, it shouldn't be difficult," Steve said. "I'm flying from here to Chicago O'Hare and from there on a commuter flight to Sioux City. Then a rent car about 50 miles north to Orange City. That's the county seat. And I'm betting Gideon's farm is around there somewhere."

CHAPTER 23

Steve parked near the courthouse in Orange City, Iowa. It was an elegant red-brick building with white stone serving as trim around the windows and along one side a tower that loomed over the area. The grand old style of a different day, Steve reflected.

The grounds that surrounded the structure were neatly manicured. Steve climbed the steps and went in search of the county recorder's office. There he was introduced to a woman named Marge whose specialty was "records research."

He stated his case. "I'm looking for someone with the last name Glenn. An address or phone number. It's a genealogy mission. Specifically, I'm trying to find anyone related to a man named Gideon Glenn, who fought in the Civil War and later settled on a farm somewhere in this county."

"That could be a pretty tall order," she said. "Our records include a growing number of farms that are absentee owned. The descendants of this man may not live on the farm any more. And may not own the property any more, for that matter. But maybe you can find your man Gideon in the files. I can show you how to search for him."

It didn't take long for Steve to cruise through the county's computerized jungle, and he did turn up property recorded in the name of Glenn. Three such names. But no Gideon.

Marge looked up when he approached her desk. "Any luck?"

"Nothing immediate," he said. "Finding the original owner is not always that easy, I guess. In any event, I found no Gideon Glenn."

"Well, sometimes the handwriting gets in the way. Some signatures are hard to read, and some people use initials that you might not be familiar with."

"I wonder," Steve said. "Do you suppose the public library here might have some sort of record of those in the county who fought in the Civil War?"

"It's possible. It's a good library. Right down the main drag. You can't miss it."

Steve pulled into the parking area alongside the Orange City Public Library and wondered if he was making any progress. Gideon Glenn had eluded him so far, but perhaps a library right here in Gideon's home territory could provide some answers.

He approached a man behind the counter in the genealogy department, stated his mission, and added, "I'm hopeful you can direct me to a list of those men in Sioux County who were veterans of the Civil War."

The worker eyed the surrounding files. "I've never seen such a compilation, but there's a wealth of information here about Iowa's role in the Civil War."

He led Steve to a file drawer marked "Sioux County" and opened it. "This is a good place to start. If you hit any snags, just let me know."

After a while Steve returned to the counter. "I don't seem to be getting any closer," he said. "Any other suggestions?"

"Well, one thought. If you don't find anything in here, there's the 1895 Iowa state census. It has a listing of 'members of household in the Civil War,' and includes the company and regiment. And also includes the state the man enlisted in if he wasn't from Iowa, as you said was the case with the man you're looking for."

"The 1895 Iowa state census? I wonder where I could get that information?"

"Well, for sure you could get it by going to the state offices in Des Moines. Otherwise, I'm not so sure. One thing certain – it's a huge list. Nearly 80,000 men served from Iowa."

"Really? That's an awful lot of farm boys, and the state must have been sparsely populated back then."

"Right on both counts," the librarian said. "Matter of fact, right after Ft. Sumter was fired on the governor of Iowa got a telegram from Lincoln requesting that the state furnish one regiment of men. And he reportedly said to his staff, 'A whole regiment! How can we do that?' Well, in the next four years the state supplied 48 infantry regiments, plus some cavalry regiments and artillery batteries. And when the war ended more than 12,000 of them were dead."

"You sound like an authority on this subject,"Steve said.

"Well, we get a number of inquiries about the Civil War. And just recently a bunch of kids working on a high school project to do with the Civil War descended on us. They had plenty of questions. Believe me, they were starting from scratch."

"I know how they feel," Steve said. "Well, I've made note of a couple of families by the name of Glenn who are living in this county. I might check them out next. Otherwise, there's that state census list you mentioned. But I still think I can find a county list of Civil War veterans somewhere."

"That reminds me," the librarian said. "There's a Civil war monument in the Ireton Cemetery that you might be interested in. It lists the names of Civil War veterans who are buried in that cemetery. Quite a number of them. We were there visiting a gravesite some years ago. You know, that's another thought – checking cemetery records around here."

"Ireton? Where's that?"

"Just a few miles west of here. Take Highway 10, and head south at the Ireton exit. I'd start at the city clerk's office there. They have files on the area. Also they can direct you to a farm family by the name of Glenn some ways outside of Ireton, and point you the right way for a visit to the cemetery."

When Steve left the Ireton city clerk's office he couldn't help but wonder about those early settlers in northwest Iowa. The hardships they had endured. What kept them from giving up and leaving shortly after they got there?

The lone fellow in the office was a local history buff and enjoyed sharing his knowledge.

And he began painting a picture of what it was like back then, when Steve inquired about settlers in the early to mid-1870's.

Yes, many log houses were built in the area in the mid 1870's, he said. Some of the settlers were homesteaders and some buyers. The going rate was around $2 an acre. It was a lonely existence. Neighbors were very scarce, and breaking up the prairie sod and planting crops was difficult.

And then, he said, came the grasshoppers, some time in the Seventies. In more than one year grasshoppers destroyed most of the crops, and there were accounts of "a huge cloud that fairly blotted out the sun."

And then came the cold, and the settlers were ill prepared for it. When the thermometer dropped to 30 below zero, sometimes as low as 40 below, they suffered. Those doing their chores couldn't stand to be outdoors. Water would freeze in a pail on the way to the house.

The city clerk also told Steve about how they would set up markers from house to shed and other buildings so as to get to their stock. In a blinding snowstorm you could freeze to death not far from your door if you lost your way. Sometimes settlers had to use corn for fuel, which they considered almost a sin. They would try to make a bushel of corn last a day in a cook stove.

Survival became a question mark when grasshoppers destroyed the crops. On the other hand, he said, putting food on the table was not always that difficult. Wild prairie chickens were plentiful, as were geese and ducks. Also, deer roamed the area, and settlers found evidence that herds of buffalo had been there at some earlier time.

There were also many foxes and wolves. And, Steve learned, the mail traveled to Ireton three times a week from Orange City, back in those days. Also in the miscellaneous category he learned that homesteaders didn't have to pay taxes on their property until they owned it outright.

As for records, the Town Hall had detailed records on births, place of birth, parents and their birthplace, and cause of death, dating back to 1890. But no mention of anyone named Gideon Glenn in the records. There was, though, the one Glenn family in the area who the librarian had mentioned to Steve. The name was Edwin Glenn.

It was worth a try, but Steve decided to take a look first at that Civil war monument he had heard about.

Steve headed for the Pleasant Hill Cemetery and pulled into the parking area inside the gate. Surveying the scene, he noted how quiet it was – not a sound. No traffic, no horns honking, no sirens, just a stillness and a light breeze rustling through the trees.

The cemetery rose up a gentle hill into the distance, and Steve started along a walkway that seemed to bisect the property. He wondered if there was by any chance a tombstone bearing the name GLENN somewhere nearby. It would be hard to find without some local knowledge.

Continuing up the walk Steve finally saw the monument the worker had mentioned in the library. It was of impressive size, maybe 15 feet tall including a Union soldier atop the monument. The soldier, with musket in hand, was standing at parade rest in full military attire, and he surveyed the countryside from atop the hill, farmland dead ahead of him and the town to his left and right.

Reaching the monument Steve read the inscription that greeted him as he came up the walkway:

"To the memory of the men who fought for our country

and are buried in the Ireton Cemetery ….. 1861-1865."

Steve turned to the list of Civil War veterans on the adjoining side and started reading downward. There were 24 names inscribed on the stone. He came to the eighth name on the list:

FISHER, ALFRED, then

FOLLETT, CHARLES J., and next

FOSBURG, PORTER

And then he saw it:

GLENN, GIDEON.

CHAPTER 24

Steve headed down the gravel road outside Ireton and was glad his rental car had a compass. The fellow in the city clerk's office had given him directions as to how to reach the farm home of Edwin Glenn, but it required negotiating a network of rural roads, mostly gravel, and not many markers.

And unlike the state highways Steve had encountered earlier, these rural roads did a bit of meandering here and there. The state roads leading into the area were hard-surface, in excellent condition and tended to follow section lines, with little deviation. If you were heading west it was due west, and it stayed that way.

Why, Steve wondered, was this road he was traveling called Dove Avenue? It was hardly an avenue. He'd forgotten how much dust a car can kick up traveling a gravel road on a dry day. He couldn't recall being on a gravel road since he was a kid.

He was much impressed by the miles of corn and soybeans he was seeing to the left and right of him. He'd never seen corn quite like this. The center on a basketball team could hide in these rows.

Steve got to wondering about the family up ahead on the Glenn farm. The fellow in the city clerk's office had said there had been Glenns on that property as far back as he could remember, and he had gone to school with Edwin Glenn. He recalled that Edwin's father, now deceased, was named Samuel, but he didn't know any others in the family.

After a right turn off Dove Avenue, then a left, then back to the right again, Steve found the Glenn home, nestled in a little grove of trees, not far from the road. The trees were there for a wind break, Steve figured. Someone had planted them. Surveying the landscape there were few trees in sight anywhere else.

Steve noted there was no livestock anywhere to be seen. But in and around a pair of nearby storage sheds was a raft of farm equipment, including a large combine that sported an enclosed cab with a windshield almost on the same level as a second-story building. This farm operator apparently worked a sizable acreage.

A series of metal grain bins stood nearby, loaded or ready to be loaded with corn and soybeans for future delivery. And close by was a large wagon and an auger used to load the grain trucks. The auger towered over the other equipment. What a departure, Steve thought, from the days when settlers picked corn by hand and dumped the ears into a shoulder bag.

He noted that the interior of one of the sheds looked like a mechanic's garage, with a cement floor and automotive and workshop equipment lining the walls. This was not a mom-and-pop operation.

Steve turned away from the equipment sheds and was admiring the huge combine when he spotted a man in kakhis and field boots coming around the side of the Glenn residence. The man sported a cap bearing the label, "Iowa State Cyclones."

"Are you in the market for a combine?" he asked.

"Don't believe so," Steve said. "But I think if would be fun to operate that baby."

"It's okay to ride in it for an hour or so. Then it gets boring. You get to thinking about other things you need to do. What can I do for you?"

"A couple of questions," Steve said. "My name is Glenn, incidentally, and I'm wondering if you are by any chance Edwin Glenn?"

"Another Glenn, huh? Yes, I am Edwin Glenn."

Steve got to the point. "The reason I'm here – I'm on a genealogy mission. Are you by any chance related to a man named Gideon Glenn?"

"Yes, he was my great-grandfather. He homesteaded this land. Why are you asking?"

Steve went on. "And he was a Civil War veteran, out of New York State?"

"Yes. I have a framed certificate in my office dating back to the late 1800's certifying that he was in a New York regiment during the war."

"Was it by any chance the 146th Regiment?"

"That sounds like it. Believe it was called the 146th Regiment, New York State Volunteers. What is your involvement here?"

"This will come as a bit of a shock to you," Steve said, "but I can explain. You see, Gideon Glenn was also *my* great grandfather."

CHAPTER 25

Saturday, and Steve and Linda Stearns were strolling along the shore at Wrightsville Beach, following the 12-mile drive from Wilmington.

"It was good of you to call me about locating Gideon," Linda said. "I was hoping you'd come back here but until you called I wasn't sure you would."

"Well, first off, I had to call you," Steve said. "Gideon is your relative, too, you know."

Linda laughed. "Yes, he is, now that you mention it. But I thought you'd be fixing to move on, now that you've found him."

"Well, I'm not quite done yet," Steve said.

Their stroll along the white sandy beach brought them to a resort, several stories of modern design stretching out along the shoreline. The rooms, Steve noted, had

floor-to-ceiling glass, and balconies, that provided an inviting view of the Atlantic.

Eyeing the structure, Steve said, "Now a land-lubber would have a hard time beating a room on the top floor of that place."

"Very nice, all right," said Linda. "But a bit pricey, I'm afraid, for my bank account." She looked at Steve. "So, I suppose now you'll be on the lookout for a job again. What was it you said – newspaper work? Or was it advertising?"

"A bit of both," Steve said. "Fresh out of college I was in the newspaper business for quite a while, then went to work for an ad agency in St. Louis. Liked what I was doing on the news side, but advertising was a big step up, dollar-wise. So I decided to spread my wings."

"Did you like the work? Advertising, that is?"

"Oh sure. It was productive work. And rewarding. We were always swamped. That is, until our main account got in trouble, and suddenly the party was over."

Just past the hotel Steve noted the west side of the resort overlooked the intracoastal waterway. The waterway had widened into a harbor at this point, which provided a place for an anchorage close to the hotel.

"Let's go back there and take a look," Steve said. "I'm not sure whether I want a room on the top floor overlooking the Atlantic or on the other side watching the boats go by."

As they approached the anchorage at the waterway Linda said, "I would vote for this side. The water looks bluer over here."

A charter boat just returning from a deep sea fishing trip was tying up, and the fishermen were busy unloading what appeared to be a sizable catch.

"What do you suppose they got into?" Steve asked.

"Well, they're not hauling up any large tuna," Linda said. "Maybe some striped bass?"

"I'll go ask."

Back up from the dock, Steve said, "They have a nice catch of Spanish mackerel and bluefish. They stayed busy out there. What say we go back around the building and visit that oceanfront dining room?"

At a table looking out on the Atlantic, Steve said, "Sounds as though you've had some experience as a saltwater angler. Any offshore fishing?"

Linda laughed. "No, no. Much closer to home. When I was young my dad would occasionally take me fishing. We would go to one of his favorite spots close to the wetlands or along a canal, and I would bottomfish mostly."

"And you put meat on the table?"

"Well, there were always sand trout and croaker to be caught. And sometimes I would catch a nice flounder. Those were trips I really looked forward to. But they were short-lived. My dad died while I was still quite young."

"So, when did you move to Wilmington?"

"I've been in and out. I worked a while in Wilmington for a title company, then my mother grew ill and I moved back to Castle Hayne to be with her. She's gone now, and I'm back."

Linda put down her menu. "Did you reach your aunt back home and tell her the news? 'Babe?'"

"That's right. 'Babe' is what she answers to. Yes, I reached her and she's on cloud nine. This closes the book on her family tree and gives her a new family tree to play with. She'll probably add a whole chapter on the 'Man from the Fifth Oneida.' And she's already talked to a couple of the gals among the Glenns up there in Iowa."

"So, now that you've found what you were looking for, what's next in your plans?"

"Well, it's time to look for a job," Steve said. "But the search may not take me far."

"Oh?"

"Not really. I'm leaving tomorrow for a couple of days. Going down to Myrtle Beach. You remember I mentioned a Civil War 'pen pal'? Barney Pollard? He's big in a Civil War Roundtable down there, and he wants me to be at their meeting tomorrow night to tell them all about how I found my missing ancestor."

"You've got quite a story to tell," Linda said. "It will get their attention, I'm sure."

"Well, I'm not sure what I'll encounter there. These 'Roundtables' are scattered across the country, and they have quite a following. And some of the people are pretty knowledgeable. A few could classify as scholars. Anyway, it should be interesting."

"And then you're coming back here?"

"Oh yes. There's another reason I'm going to Myrtle Beach. Maybe you've heard of Dillard News. I had the good fortune to meet Frank Dillard recently, and he's called to see if I'd be interested in going to work for him. I'm meeting him down there day after tomorrow."

Linda's eyes lit up. "Really! Would it be work on a newspaper? That is, on the 'news side'? Or advertising?"

"Both," Steve said. "I don't know all the details yet, but from what Frank Dillard said about it, I'm interested. I think you know, I like it in this part of the world. For a number of reasons." He glanced out over the water, then back at Linda. "You're one of the reasons, you know."

Steve motioned for a waiter, then back at Linda. "For the moment let's just say, if it's a good offer I'll take it."

Linda smiled. "That would be nice."

Would you like to see your manuscript become a book?

If you are interested in becoming a PublishAmerica author, please submit your manuscript for possible publication to us at:

acquisitions@publishamerica.com

You may also mail in your manuscript to:

**PublishAmerica
PO Box 151
Frederick, MD 21705**

We also offer free graphics for Children's Picture Books!

---

www.publishamerica.com

CPSIA information can be obtained at www.ICGtesting.com
Printed in the USA
LVOW12s2020190913

353252LV00001B/120/P